REZ
REBEL

REZ REBEL

MELANIE FLORENCE

JAMES LORIMER & COMPANY LTD., PUBLISHERS
TORONTO

James Lorimer & Company Ltd., Publishers acknowledges funding support from the Ontario Arts Council (OAC), an agency of the Government of Ontario. We acknowledge the support of the Canada Council for the Arts, which last year invested $153 million to bring the arts to Canadians throughout the country. This project has been made possible in part by the Government of Canada and with the support of the Ontario Media Development Corporation.

 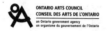

Cover design: Tyler Cleroux
Cover images: Shutterstock

Library and Archives Canada Cataloguing in Publication

Florence, Melanie, author
       Rez rebel / Melanie Florence.

Issued in print and electronic formats.
ISBN 978-1-4594-1199-9 (paperback).--ISBN 978-1-4594-1201-9 (epub)

       I. Title.

PS8611.L668R485 2017   jC813.6   C2016-906042-X
                                                C2016-906043-8

Published by: Distributed by:
James Lorimer & Company Ltd.,   Formac Lorimer Books
Publishers   5502 Atlantic Street
117 Peter Street, Suite 304   Halifax, NS, Canada
Toronto, ON, Canada   B3H 1G4
M5V 0M3
www.lorimer.ca

Printed and bound in Canada.
Manufactured by Friesens Corporation in Altona, Manitoba, Canada in March 2017.
Job #231495

For Josh and Taylor.
And for Kat, who has made me a better writer.

A NOTE
FROM THE AUTHOR

Suicide among young people, especially in Indigenous communities, is a problem that needs talking, writing, and reading about. And the language we use to do this is important. Studies and history have shown that having First Nations kids learn hereditary languages and culture is a major way to prevent suicide. In this story, Floyd and his friends and parents speak English, but also use Cree words and terms. Because it is natural for these characters to speak the Cree language, the words are not set apart from the rest of the text. But here are the Cree terms used and their English translations:

maskosis — little bear or bear cub
miwapewiw — he is handsome
miyo kisikaw — it is a fine day
miyo takosin — good evening or it is a fine night
nimosôm — my grandfather
pe mitso — come and eat
tânisi — Hello. How are you?
wâpos — rabbit

Chapter 1
IN THE WOODS

BIRTH OF A WARRIOR

Floyd Twofeathers was born in a teepee in an overgrown forest when the moon was at its fullest, looking over the Bitter Lake Reserve. He was born into a long line of Chiefs and Medicine Women and a tribe of warriors.

I had always wanted to be a writer. So I guess it was in my nature to be poetic, maybe overly poetic. The bio I wrote would have been really cool if I had come into this world in, say, the 1800s. But in fact I was born in the early '00s. That's 2000s, not 1900s. I came into being in the decade that brought us the iPhone, reality TV, and UFC. It might have been the twenty-first century, but Indians — or Indigenous Canadians if you want to be politically correct — were still stuck with stereotypes. Stereotypes like alcoholism and abuse, or images that included buffalo hunting with a bow and arrow. I'm actually pretty good with a bow and arrow. But there are no buffalo for me to hunt. And I would much rather watch animals than hunt them. My weapon of choice is a notebook and pen. You know, the pen is mightier than the sword and all that. I never go anywhere without a notebook and pen — tools of my trade — in my back pocket. As for that other stereotype? I never touch the stuff.

It was quiet in the forest. There was only the rustle of the wind through the trees. I heard the sound of birds chirping and the soft flutter of their wings as they moved from branch to branch. I could even make out the crush of leaves beneath the feet of the animals. A rabbit crept out from under a bush. Nose twitching, the rabbit hopped past and disappeared back into the forest. I waited . . . breathing quietly . . . as still as the trees around me. The late August sun was beating mercilessly on the back of my neck, turning my skin an even darker shade of brown.

I watched my mother gathering ingredients for her medicines. My mom, Cardinal Twofeathers, is a healer, a medicine woman from a long line of medicine women. I was eager to learn all I could from her. She taught me to respect Mother Earth. She taught me about sacred medicines and how to speak our language. She told me stories my entire life, our history and our folklore. And she encouraged me to write my own stories down.

"There's a lot to be learned in the forest, Maskosis," she would tell me. She used her favourite nickname for me — Little Bear. Yes, I was her little bear. I was always by her side while I was growing up, quick to learn about the roots she would dig up and the leaves she would boil for teas that would cure everything from colds to stomach ache.

I sat down against a tree trunk and pulled out my notebook, flipping through until I found an empty page.

Dear Diary

Ugh. No. That sounded like I was a ten-year-old girl or something.

That wasn't much better. I stared down at the blank page. Why did it have to be "Dear" something? That was way too formal. I chewed on the end of my pen thoughtfully. I glanced at my mother digging up roots and wondered what I could write about her. How would I describe her to someone who didn't know her?

She's a lot smarter than me. And she's beautiful in a way that makes men stop and stare at her when we go into the city. I've always hated that. Women are drawn to her for her kindness and knowledge. I spend hours with her in the forest or in the kitchen, cooking dinner. I guess you could call me a mama's boy. But if my mother is the mama in question, it doesn't seem like an insult to me.

I was brought out of my reverie by a satisfied sigh from my mom. She sat back on her heels, holding a long piece of bark in her dirty hands. She brushed it off on her pants and smiled, holding it out to me. She wanted me to tell her what it was. It was a game we played often, a test to see how much I had learned from her, how much I could remember.

"Well, Maskosis? Do you recognize this one?"

I frowned for a moment, letting her think she had me stumped. Then a grin slid across my face as I caught her eye. She wasn't fooled for a second.

"Quaking Aspen," I answered, shoving my notebook back into my pocket.

"And what is it used for?"

"The inner bark is used as a poultice for dressing wounds," I shot back. She smiled, clearly pleased. I caught the familiar scents of sweetgrass, sage, and cedar. Each of those plants was used so often and for so many different medicines that the smell of them clung to my mother like a perfume. I couldn't ever smell those scents without thinking of her. Traditional. Steeped in the culture of our people. Proud of who she was and where she came from.

"Floyd?" My mother's soft voice interrupted my daydream. "Where did you go?"

"Sorry. I'm here. Did you get everything you need?"

"Yes. I'm going to boil the roots tonight and make a poultice for Auntie Martha. She's had that cough for weeks and it hasn't gotten any better. Maybe you can run it over for me tomorrow with some of Raynetta's chicken soup?"

"Yeah, sure. I'm going past there with the guys tomorrow morning anyway."

"Thank you." She raised a hand and I helped her to her feet. She tossed her leather pouch of roots and barks to me and turned her face up toward the warm sun. She looked so young that I stood still as a statue, afraid to break the spell. I loved this side of my mom. This was the carefree, childlike version of my mother that seemed to mostly come out in the forest, where we were surrounded by all the things we both loved the most.

Chapter 2
ON THE REZ

We walked out of the woods in comfortable silence. The dense forest gave way as we reached the edge and plunged out into the full force of daylight. My pickup truck was parked at the edge of the woods. It was a jade green monster that I had worked, scrimped, and saved every penny for. I'd finally had the money to buy it that June. My truck was old, but she ran like a dream.

I opened the passenger door and held it as my mother climbed up into the cab. I closed the door, strode around to the driver's side and climbed in beside her. The ignition made a grinding noise as I turned the key. Then the engine roared into life. Damn, I loved that truck. I had been trying to think of a name for her since I got her. But I still hadn't come up with the right one. I had tried Selena (my Selena Gomez phase), Tricky (I don't remember why . . . I think one of the guys came up with that one), Cherry, Stacey, Muffin (that was Mouse's idea, he's four years younger than me), Esmerelda . . . Nope. Hadn't found the right name yet. But I knew it would come to me eventually. I patted the steering wheel as I drove away from the woods and toward home.

We cruised down the road, past the forest at the edge of the reserve, past the green hay and cornfields and into the cluster of homes. Clothes hung on lines outside. Children ran races and pummeled each other in front yards. Dogs twitched sleepily on porches. Women called out to each other, balancing chubby brown babies on their hips and waving to us as we passed. One day was the same as any other here. I loved it. I couldn't imagine living anywhere else.

Still, I knew that not everyone felt the same way. We didn't have it easy on our rez.

There weren't many jobs. There wasn't a youth program. We were bussed out for middle and high school. Most of us had been the object of some kind of racism at one point or another when we were off the rez. Some people didn't have electricity at home. And most of the people here were poor. With nothing to do and a future that was more often dark than bright, we had been seeing a pretty high number of suicides among our youth.

I had lost one of my best friends a month ago. Aaron had left a note saying that no one understood him. He thought we'd all be happier without him around. I still couldn't believe he was gone. I had ideas about why he had killed himself, but I didn't want to think about that either.

I cleared my throat and tried to clear my head too. "Mom, did you want to stop at Auntie Martha's for tea or something?"

"No, Maskosis. I have those roots to boil and dinner to start."

"Mom! Miyo kisikaw — it's a fine day! Let's go see what Raynetta's doing."

She smiled.

"Floyd, why don't you take one of those sandwiches in the cooler to your father, then go see the boys?" She was clearly trying to get me out of her hair for a while.

"Yeah, okay." I pulled up in front of our house.

"Be home for dinner?" she asked as she ruffled my hair.

"Of course."

I watched her pick up the bag of roots and walk into the house.

The band office was in a small building that also housed a tiny library with books that were sadly out of date. I kept meaning to organize a book drive or ask my high school if they had any to donate. The building also held our medical centre. It was a bit of a joke because we had just one nurse on site. A doctor came in once a week or so. But he didn't put in nearly enough hours to see everyone who needed his care. There was also a dental office, which was what we called the one room for the visiting dentist. It was a lot like living in the old west, actually. The only thing we were missing was a travelling judge.

A few years ago, the council had made plans for a whole new medical centre. It would have a full-time doctor and nurse on staff, plus a full-time dentist. It would have a diabetes clinic. A shrink would be on call. It would barely cover the needs of the rez, but it was a start.

The council couldn't come up with the funding.

I walked in and headed toward my father's office. It was quiet in the building today. And empty. I knew my dad would be in his office, buried behind a pile of paperwork. He was probably applying for some kind of grant. I don't know how he did it. He kept asking for money to get us what we needed. And he kept getting turned down.

I heard my dad clearing his throat when I was still out in the hallway. I was about to call out a greeting. Then I caught a glimpse of him through the door and came to a sudden stop. My father is usually animated and confident. But today he was sitting slump-shouldered with his head in his hands.

I'm not an idiot. There was a lot of pressure on my father to fix all of the problems on the rez. And with the suicides that had been happening, I knew he had more than his share of stress. But I had rarely seen him looking as tired and helpless as he did at that moment.

If my mother was quietly strong and sure, my father was the exact opposite. Victor Twofeathers was an imposing figure. He was tall, muscular, and outspoken with a boisterous laugh and a charming way about him. His manner drew people in and made them want to be around him. He was firm but kind, imposing yet inviting. People loved him but feared him a little. I had thought about it enough to figure out what made him that way.

My father had spent six years in a residential school, his own father before him even longer. My father rarely talked about it. But I had heard horror stories growing up on the rez. If they were even just partly true, then my father had been to hell and back. Being forced to deny his culture and to be ashamed of who he was and where he came from was the least of what he would have gone through. Every conceivable kind of abuse took place at those schools. It was hard to believe that my big, confident father had been through that. I couldn't imagine anyone ever getting the best of him. I just couldn't wrap my head around it. How do you put that kind of thing behind you and live a normal life? But he had done it. I admired him for that. So many other survivors drowned in addictions, unable to move past their abuse. But my dad refused to touch booze or drugs, and did the best he could as chief.

He's actually the hereditary chief. That means that his position has been passed down from generation to generation. We're a self-governing reserve, so he acts as elected chief too.

No one else wanted the job, not with all the issues we've been facing. Lack of clean water. Suicide. Alcoholism. Poverty. Drug abuse. No one else wanted to be the one who has to answer all the questions. So my father stepped up and serves as Chief Councilman along with two others on the council. I'll inherit the job someday.

Chapter 3
FAMILY

I took several steps away from the office and made a big noisy show of approaching the door the second time. When I reached the doorway this time, my dad was shuffling papers around his desk. He looked up and smiled, nodding at the bundle in my hands.

"Is that for me?" he asked.

"Hey, Dad." I put the sandwich and a thermos of coffee down on his desk and sat in the only other chair in the room. Actually, there was a third chair. But it had been covered in books and papers for as long as I could remember. You couldn't see it unless you already knew it was there.

I looked at my dad closely. There was no trace of the mood I had caught him in just a moment before. A smudge of ink marked his cheek. "Floyd," he said, as if checking my name off a list. "Your mom send you over?"

I nodded toward the sandwich. "She wanted to make sure you ate something." In answer to his smile, I asked, "What are you doing?"

"Trying to figure out how to get the government to set up a filtration system. We're this close to getting hit with a boil water advisory." He held up his fingers with the smallest space between them and sighed. Our water *had* been looking kind of brown. But so far, it was still safe to drink. My father was working day and night to try to get it cleaned up before we had to boil it before drinking it. Just one more thing he had on his plate.

"Anything I can help with?" I asked. I already knew the answer. Although I was to be the next hereditary chief, my father still thought I was too young to do anything useful.

"No, not really. Why don't you go and play with your friends?" he suggested. He looked back down at his desk, the message clear. *Did he just tell me to go play? Really?*

"Yeah, sure." I stood up and headed toward the door. "See you at home?"

"Uh huh." His mind was already back in his work.

I knew my dad had a fun side to him. It just didn't come out much anymore. He spent so much time working that he didn't have time for us like he used to.

With eight years between them, my parents might not have had much to talk about if they lived in the city. But on the rez, culture and tradition go a long way. My mother was a traditional Cree woman. Even as a teenager, she knew how to care for a home and a family. She could cook, clean, and sew. She could plant a garden and grow her own vegetables. She had helped raise her four brothers and sisters. She had worked with and learned from Mary Running Wolf. Mary was a healer who people came from all over to see.

My mother married my father when she was eighteen. Dad first laid eyes on her at a community dance at his rez. She was visiting family. He swept her off her feet. He was a full-grown man. He was strong and sure. What more could a girl want?

I used to imagine what my parents' first meeting must have been like. They would have been young and my dad wouldn't have lost his soul in the council office yet.

*Fade in on a girl, standing behind a table laden with food.
She is smiling shyly at people as she hands out napkins
of cookies and ladles out fruit punch. She pushes a braid
over her shoulder and glances wistfully around at the
people dancing. Maybe she wishes that someone would
ask her to dance.*

*A man steps up to the table, surrounded by his friends. He's
handsome but he shows no interest in the girls fluttering
around him and his group. He's clearly the leader of the
gang. People flock around him, as if some of what makes
him stand out might rub off on them. He stops in front of
the girl and smiles down at her.*

Victor: Hi. I'm Victor. I don't think we've met.

The girl colours slightly. But she smiles back.

Cardinal: No. I'm just here visiting my aunt.

Victor: Aren't you going to tell me your name?

*She laughs. It's a tinkling, magical sound. Victor is instantly
transfixed.*

Cardinal: I'm Cardinal.

*Now Victor's entire group of friends is staring at the girl as
well. There's just something about her. But the rest of them
don't stand a chance. Not with Victor there.*

Victor: (tilting his head and studying her) I think you may be the prettiest girl here, Cardinal.

She blushes and picks up a cookie, holding it out to him.

Cardinal: Would you like a cookie?

Victor: (smiling) No. But I'd love a dance.

He holds out his hand. She takes it and steps around the food table. Victor wraps an arm around her and pulls her in close.

It's cheesy, I know. But I was trying my hand at writing romantic comedy at the time.

Since my dad had no use for me, I headed back home. Maybe my mom would want me to take her to visit Auntie Martha that night. I jumped out of the truck and took the front steps two at a time. If I hurried, I'd still be able to meet the guys and get some work done on the car we had all chipped in to buy. It was a piece-of-crap beater, probably bright red once but now faded to kind of a rusty orange. We had been working on it for months and finally had it running. But there were still some tweaks we had to make before we could really drive it. I figured today we'd be able to finish tuning it up.

The phone rang while I was busy looking for a snack in the fridge. I heard my mom answer in the other room. After a few minutes, she walked into the kitchen and put a hand on my shoulder. I was washing an apple at the sink and barely looked up.

"Floyd?"

Her voice sounded odd. I turned and looked at her. Her face was white as paper.

"Mom? Are you okay?" I led her to the kitchen table and eased her into one of the chairs. "Tea?" It was the only thing I could think to say or do.

She shook her head.

"No. Sit down, son." She held my hands as I sat down in front of her.

"Mom? What is it?" I had never seen her like this. Her hands shook in mine. Her eyes were swimming with tears. "Mom? You're scaring me."

"Five girls made some kind of a pact. They tried to kill themselves last night," she said. Her voice was shaking almost as badly as her hands.

"What? What do you mean, a pact?" Had I heard that right?

"A suicide pact. Three are dead. They're only twelve and thirteen years old." She drew a breath that caught in her throat. "Two of them are still alive. One is Theresa's granddaughter."

Theresa was our next door neighbour. I had known her my entire life. Her granddaughter, Summer, was five years younger than me. But on the same rez everyone knew everyone else, no matter what age. Summer always had a smile on her face as she spent time with her grandmother, helping with housework and gardening. I couldn't match that smiling little girl with a kid who wanted to end her life.

"Is she going to be okay?"

"I don't know. I'm going over to Theresa's now to take her to the hospital." She looked at me, pushing the hair off my face. "Those poor girls," she murmured, shaking her head.

Five of them? No doubt I knew them all. Why would kids so young want to end their lives?

"If you ever . . . if you felt like that, Floyd . . . you'd tell me, wouldn't you?" she asked.

"I'd never do anything like try to kill myself, Mom." I stood up and gave her a hug that nearly lifted her off the floor. "Go and take care of Theresa."

She nodded and gathered up some things. She had grabbed her purse and gone out the door by the time I realized I hadn't even asked her who the other girls were. I'd find out soon enough. If it happened last night, then everyone would already be talking about it.

Chapter 4
THE PACT

I pushed my braid back over my shoulder out of habit. *A suicide pact?* I shook my head. I'd never be able to understand how anyone could feel that desperate and hopeless. How bad did it have to be that they couldn't imagine things ever getting better? My life might not be perfect but it always got better in time. Always. I'd never once considered taking a gun out to the woods and ending things.

But Aaron did.

I shook my head, trying to get rid of the mental image. The guys would be waiting for me, already talking about the suicides, I was sure. We lived in a community where nothing much ever happened or changed. A suicide pact would have everyone buzzing.

I thought about it and realized that mom had been getting more and more calls like this one. Not suicide pact calls, thank god. But calls from families grieving for their children. Calls about kids who had taken a way out that I couldn't begin to wrap my mind around.

I wondered if any of my friends had thought about it. Other than Aaron, I mean. I hadn't even known he was depressed. I had a sudden need to talk to every one of my friends and ask how they were.

I grabbed my phone and sent a text to Jasper and Charlie, asking what was up. I could have just met up with them and asked in person, but I didn't want to wait that long. To be honest, I didn't really feel like hanging out anymore.

As I waited for the familiar ding to alert me to an incoming text, I logged in to my Instagram account. I noticed I was tagged in a bunch of photos. I clicked idly through. A couple looked the same. Photos of a laptop screen with text. I stopped and read what it said, losing my breath as I scanned the words. I clicked through a couple more of the photos I had been tagged in.

When it hit me what I was seeing, I felt like I had been kicked in the stomach. Each of the girls who had been part of the suicide pact had posted the photo of their note on Instagram.

They sit in a circle around the laptop, staring intently at the screen. The eerie glow lights their faces in the darkened room. There are five of them, all girls with dark hair and eyes that are too haunted for ones so young. They read the words together. Some move their lips. Some look at the screen without blinking.

"To Whom It May Concern,

Hell is being a teenaged girl with no future, no life outside of a tiny place that has nothing to offer. All we can expect is teen pregnancy and, if we're lucky, a minimum wage job as a cashier.

To our families: we love you. But maybe our absence will make your own lives a little easier. Don't blame

*yourselves. You couldn't have stopped us and you didn't
do anything wrong."*

*They each take a turn at the keyboard, signing their names
with no hesitation.*

Katie
Sara
Nicole
Anna
Summer

I chewed on the end of my pen and frowned. I had
been trying to imagine what had gone through their heads
last night. But I didn't want think about Summer as being
hopeless. I didn't want to think about any of the other girls like that.
I turned the page and tried again.

THE FIVE PRINCESSES — by Floyd Twofeathers

*Once upon a time there were five princesses. They lived in
the tower of a castle; a fortress where nothing and no one
could ever get in or out.*

*For a long time, the girls were happy in their tower. They had
everything they were used to and the stories they told one
another. And they had each other. But as they got older, it was
no longer enough for them. They started wondering what they
were missing. What was outside the walls of their castle?*

"I wish we could play outside," one of them said.

"I wish we had more friends," said another.

"I wish there were other people who could listen to our stories," sighed another.

"I wish we could do whatever we wanted to do," one of the girls said.

The girls looked at each other. They began arguing about all of the things they felt sure they were missing out on. They forgot about their beautiful home. They didn't know how dangerous the world outside the tower could be.

Finally, they decided to venture out of their home and explore. They would look for whatever would make them the happiest in the world.

The five princesses searched desperately for a way out of their tower. But the only door was locked tightly. It didn't move even a little when they put all their weight against it. No matter how they pushed or pulled, the door didn't budge.

The only way out of the tower was through the window set in the wall. It looked over endless forests and streams.

They walked together to the window and looked down.

"It's so high," one of the princesses said. She gulped nervously.

"Too high," said another. She shook her head.

"We'll die if we jump out," said one princess. She clutched the beaded necklace around her throat.

"We'll die if we don't," said the fourth princess. "I can't stay in this tower another minute. I can't breathe in here." She climbed slowly onto the window ledge, shrugging off the fifth girl's hand. She stood there, looking down. "It's not that high," she said. She took a deep breath and jumped.

The other princesses leaned out the window in a tangle of gowns and limbs. They watched as their sister fell to the ground and landed heavily. They watched as she lay still, not moving. They called out to her but there was no reply.

"She may not have made it," the princess who had been holding her sister's hand said. "But that doesn't mean I won't." And with that, she threw herself out the window. She landed beside her sister. There she lay, still as a shadow.

"Wait for me!" cried the princess with the necklace. She held out her arms as if she could fly and jumped. Instead of soaring, she fell to the ground.

Three princesses lay motionless on the stones surrounding the tower. The other two looked down at them.

"I don't want to stay here," one of them said. "But I'm afraid of falling."

"Me too," the other girl replied, gripping her hand tightly.

"Perhaps we should jump together." The princess looked down sadly at her sisters who had escaped the tower.

"Or maybe we should stay," the other remaining girl said.

"I'm afraid to jump. But I'm afraid to stay too."

The other nodded. Neither option seemed right at that moment. But there was no third choice.

The girls held hands tightly. They stepped up onto the windowsill. They looked far below where their sisters lay. They looked back into the tower.

They took a deep breath and jumped. Together. Hands clasped.

Chapter 5
DINNER AT HOME

I closed my notebook slowly. I slid my hand over it, feeling the well-worn cover under my fingers. I couldn't really find the words to talk about so many things, but I could always write it down. I was grateful for that. Writing helped me work out a lot of things. Getting my thoughts down on paper — even when it was just a story I made up — somehow made it a little easier to deal with.

I walked into the kitchen and noticed the sink full of dishes from breakfast. They had been left soaking but my mom had to leave before she could get to them.

As I emptied the sink and then refilled it with soapy water, I thought about how tired my mom and dad had been lately. Neither of them was getting much sleep. I knew that their jobs as medicine woman and chief were exhausting in the best of times. And this wasn't the best of times. Not even close. How could they heal and lead a community that couldn't find the will to get better or move forward?

I knew the guys were expecting me to come by. And I really wanted to hang out with them; get some work done on the beater. But I figured maybe there was something I could do to make life a little easier for my parents. Even if it was just for one night.

I spent the next hour chopping and sautéing. I made a huge mess of the kitchen. My mom had taught me how to cook when I was a kid. I usually griped a bit when I was asked to whip something up, but she knew as much as I did that I enjoyed it. It reminded me of helping her collect the right plants and roots and combining them to make something to cure colds or fever or whatever. Cooking was to make something to feed and nourish. For both healing and cooking, getting the ingredients just right was a science.

I scrubbed the last of the breakfast dishes while the pasta and sauce bubbled on the stove. My parents walked in together, looking drained.

"Something smells good," my mom called out. She dropped her bag onto a chair and walked into the kitchen.

"Taste," I ordered, going to the stove and stirring the sauce. I held out the wooden spoon to her. She put her lips to it but I knew she wasn't really tasting it. Exhaustion and sorrow were etched into her face.

"It's perfect," she told me, trying to smile. She reached out and touched my face.

I put the spoon down.

"How's Summer? Is she going to be okay?" I asked even though I was afraid to hear the answer.

My mom pulled out a kitchen chair. She lowered herself into it carefully as though she was in pain. "I hope so. They flew her to another hospital. Her organs are badly damaged. They have to keep her in an induced coma. They won't know more until she wakes up."

"And the other girl?" I asked.

"Nicole." My mom shook her head sadly. "She didn't make it."

I slumped down beside her.

"So Nicole, Katie, Sara, and Anna are dead?" I asked. I thought my mom might ask how I knew which girls signed the pact. But I worried that telling her about the girls posting their intentions on social media would make her feel worse. She knew as well as I did that those five girls were as tight a group as my own. You rarely saw one without seeing all five. My heart hurt suddenly as I realized I'd never see the five of them together again.

Four of them gone and one in critical condition. Our children were dying one at a time.

My mom reached over and squeezed my hand. "I'll set the table," she said as my father walked into the room, hair wet from the shower.

Dad sat down and picked up the mail from the bowl in the centre of the table. He leafed through it, putting some envelopes in a pile and opening others. His reading glasses were perched on the end of his nose, threatening to slip off any second. I could tell he was going through the mail without really seeing it. He looked as drained as my mother.

"Dad?" I hated to add to his stress. But I needed to talk. He glanced up over the rims of his glasses. He looked almost startled to see me sitting across from him. I wasn't surprised. He barely noticed anything around him lately.

He raised his eyebrows at me.

"I know you've got a lot on your mind . . ." I swallowed before continuing. "But . . . I just wondered . . . is there anything I can do? To help you?" I saw him glance over at my mother before putting down his mail and taking his glasses off.

"I wish there was, son. The council is trying to bring in more money and the right people. But there's not much else you can do except this." He gestured around the kitchen. "Help out your mom.

That helps both of us." He put his glasses back on and opened another envelope.

I glanced over at my mom. "Yeah. I will. But . . . I thought . . . maybe you and I could talk?"

"Talk?" My dad glanced down, dismissing me. "Umm, yeah. Sure. Or you could talk to your mom too, you know." He stood up suddenly. "I need to get something," he said. He left the room without looking back at me.

Wow. It took him less than five seconds to shut me down and banish me from his mind.

My mom's voice broke through my thoughts. "I think the pasta is ready, Maskosis. Can you come and drain it?" she said gently.

It was pretty clear that she was trying to distract me from the fact that my father wasn't able to deal with me. Suddenly I felt a little guilty. My dad wasn't big on talking about his feelings even when things were going well for him. Why would I think that he should take on my feelings too?

I took the boiling pot of pasta off the stove and to the sink. I closed my eyes as the steam washed over me.

My mother leaned over my shoulder, tugging on my braid. "He's got a lot on his mind, Floyd," she whispered in my ear. "Your father feels responsible for what's been happening . . . the suicides and everything."

"Why?" I asked, as I dumped the pasta into a serving bowl. "It's not his fault."

"I know. But it's the hereditary chief's job to protect our people. He's supposed to preserve our culture. But he's watching it die bit by bit and that's part of the problem. He's trying to figure out how to help everyone. But he feels like nothing he is doing can turn this around."

"So what can we do to help?" I asked her.

She shook her head sadly. "I honestly don't know," she said. Then she quickly pasted on a smile as my father walked back in and sat down.

"Hey, Dad?" I began tentatively.

"Is dinner ready?" he asked.

Okay. He couldn't make it any clearer than that. He didn't want to talk about it. Maybe it just wasn't the right time. I smiled faintly at my mom and turned to finish making dinner for my family.

We steered clear of any touchy subjects as we ate. I cracked jokes and told stories about my friends. I talked about the beater and anything else I could think of. I did my best to keep them distracted from everything that was going on right outside our front door.

I cleaned up after dinner, shooing my parents out of the kitchen and refusing my mother's offer to help. They desperately needed an early night.

We all did.

Once upon a time

It was a dark and stormy night

The rez is dying.

And no one is doing anything about it.

Chapter 6
REZ BEATER

My father was rinsing his coffee cup at the sink when I walked into the kitchen the next morning. He nodded his good morning to me then leaned down to kiss my mother and whispered something in her ear. She blushed. She grabbed the dishtowel and swatted him with it. They both looked much better today . . . like they had actually gotten some sleep. And they were acting like teenagers in love. I shuddered, trying to erase that thought from my head.

Even so, I almost tried to talk to my dad again. But I stopped myself just as he turned toward me.

"Big plans today, son?" My dad smiled and stood back against the counter.

"Nah. Gonna see what the guys are doing." I handed him the newspaper and his keys. "Another day at the office, eh?"

"Another day, another dollar," he joked. He kissed my mother again, and pulled her against him. I looked away. Ew. I mean, it was nice that they were still in love after all these years. But come on. Did they have to grope each other right in front of me?

Dad gave me a quick, one-armed hug before he grabbed his lunch off of the table. I was stunned. I mean, I knew my father loved me. But he usually didn't show it with hugs.

"You should be excited about this, Floyd. The Council meeting is next week and we're planning something pretty big . . ." He trailed off as he walked toward the door. He waved over his shoulder at us and let the door slam shut behind him. My mother winced. She hated when he did that.

"What was that all about?" I asked her. "What are they planning?"

She shrugged. "I have no idea."

I grabbed an apple and kissed my mom on the cheek. "Be home later." I left, careful to let the door close gently behind me.

As I bounded down the front steps two at a time, my braids flew up and hit my cheek. I was glad I had tied my hair back. It was going to be a scorcher! But it was still early and the whole day was stretched out before me like deer hide on a drying rack. Late August and already fall was in the air. The leaves were starting to change into a dazzling array of reds, yellows and oranges. The rez was alive. I smelled fry bread sizzling in oil. I heard the sound of radios blaring hip hop music. I took in the sight of kids playing soccer, the dust rising in clouds around their shuffling feet and coating their brown skin with a thin layer of pale earth.

"Tânisi, Floyd!" The greeting came from a small figure whose lightning-fast feet were kicking up a huge cloud of dust. His frame was swimming in an old, red David Beckham jersey from the star's days with Manchester United and faded jeans at least two sizes too big. He broke away from the scrimmage and launched himself against my legs, sending me stumbling back a few steps.

"Hey, Mouse. Who's winning?" I clapped a hand on his head, messing up his already tousled hair.

"Hey!" He smoothed a hand over his head. "We're up by four."

Mouse fell into step beside me, taking two steps to my every one. He was fourteen but small for his age. I was aware that he took a lot of slack for that at school. But he was smart and funny. And he seemed to think I was someone to look up to.

We turned a corner and saw Jasper leaning back against the side of the junky old car. It barely ran and made so much noise and smoke that you feared for your life every time you got into it. Charlie's head was buried under the hood. All I could see of him were his jean-clad legs. There was a big oily stain on the back where you could tell he had been wiping his dirty hands. He was going to catch hell from his mom for that. I could hear him cursing loudly to himself as he tinkered with the engine.

"Hey, Floyd!" yelled Jasper.

"How ya doin', Jas?"

I leaned against the car and crossed one leg over the other. I got ready with my best old-timer Rez accent and jumped into storyteller mode. Storytelling has always been a big part of our culture. It was always me who came up with the good stories on the spot. They didn't always have a lesson or moral or anything but they always made my friends laugh. And at that moment, we needed laughs way more than a life lesson.

"I heard Thomas say just this morning that they were going to get the ice ready. Get the hockey team practicing for the season. Already, eh? Seems a bit early, ennit?"

"We need all the help we can get," said Mouse.

"Yeah, yeah . . . I suppose. Who ever heard of Indians playing hockey anyway, you know? It's unnatural. Should be riding horses or some shit. We're warriors, ennit? Warriors don't play sports, man!"

Mouse grinned. "Floyd, you go to every game."

"And soccer! Jeez! Don't get me started on soccer!"

"How about lacrosse, Floyd? Warriors played lacrosse, right?"

"Now you're talkin', man! Yeah. That's a real Indian sport, ennit? Did you know that the Comanche invented lacrosse, man?"

"They did not!" Mouse shot back.

"Yeah, man. Some Comanche fisherman was hanging out with his brothers, you know? And they're fishing, right? But nothing's biting. So this one guy starts waving his net around, acting stupid. And his buddy throws a rock at him because he's being such a jerk off. And he catches it in his net, man! And that's how lacrosse was invented."

Jasper joined in, smirking. "By the Comanche?"

I nodded.

Mouse's eyes were wide, his mouth hanging agape. "Is that true?" he breathed.

"No way!" said Jasper. "The Iroquois invented it. And the Comanche weren't fishermen, Floyd. They didn't even eat fish!"

"Details, man." I waved my hand carelessly in Jasper's direction, dropping the accent. Then I banged a fist on the hood. "Charlie! Haven't you gotten this piece of crap running yet?"

"It's been acting up, Floyd. The wipers keep going on by themselves. And if we keep the heater on low, it stops." He threw the keys over to me.

See what I mean? Rez beater.

Charlie stood up, wiping his hands on the back of his jeans again. Jasper walked over to look under the hood and Charlie threw an arm over his shoulder. It was a friendly enough gesture. At least it was until Charlie turned it into a headlock. Jasper yelled and clawed at Charlie's arm while Mouse and I laughed.

"Quit it, Charlie!" yelled Jasper. But Charlie had watched enough Ultimate Fighting Championships to have mastered his headlock technique. He also had a good six inches on Jasper, who topped out at five foot four. Jas insisted he was five foot six. But we had measured him while he was splayed out on Charlie's floor fast asleep a few weeks ago. And we had the pictures to prove it.

"I mean it, Charlie! I can't friggin' breathe, you ass!" choked Jas.

Charlie let him go, grinning widely. "And Jasper Janvier taps out, ladies and gentlemen," he crowed. "Charlie Trejo is still the undisputed UFC champion of the world!" He raised his arms over his head in victory as Mouse and I cheered and whistled.

Jasper punched him in the arm. "Dick," Jas grumbled, rubbing at his neck. He had just started wearing his hair gelled up into a spiky style that was clearly supposed to add that extra height he claimed we were robbing from him. Of course Charlie never missed a chance to mess up the 'do. Like me, Charlie wore his hair long, usually in a ponytail. In Charlie's case it was to keep it off a face that was often buried under the hood of the beater. I guess we all looked like all the other Indian kids on the rez. Not that a lot of us still wore our hair in braids or anything. Most of my friends kept their hair pretty short. Even so, in the city, they'd be hard pressed to tell any of us apart. They certainly couldn't or wouldn't at school. We all looked alike to most of them.

"All right, you guys," I said, before another free for all started. "Let's get going. Come on, Jas. You coming, Mouse?"

Mouse looked at me, his eyes shining and an eager look on his face. I grinned and held open the door for him.

Chapter 7
TARGET PRACTICE

Charlie yelled, "Shotgun!" and stepped quickly in front of Mouse to claim the front seat. We all knew there was less chance of choking up there. The car started with a coughing roar, belching out thick clouds of smoke. Mouse and Jasper coughed loudly in the back seat. I threw them a dark glance in the rear-view mirror and they stopped, and started laughing instead.

None of us said anything. There was no point in trying to talk over the noise coming from under the hood. And from under our feet. And from somewhere in the trunk. In fact, it sounded like there was someone in the trunk, banging to get out. I saw that Mouse looked completely unnerved in the back seat and I flashed him a smile in the rear-view mirror.

"Don't worry, man. This old car will outlive all of us." I instantly wished I could take those words back. It made me think of Aaron.

Mouse sat up straighter. "Where we goin', Floyd?"

Charlie turned around in his seat and answered for me. "My uncle's field, down at the edge of the rez." Mouse must have looked puzzled because Charlie continued. "We do target practice there."

"You have a gun?" Mouse asked, clearly impressed.

"It's my dad's," admitted Charlie. "But he doesn't mind if I borrow it as long as I replace the ammo."

I turned off the dirt road onto an even dustier laneway. It led around Charlie's uncle's cabin and past a chicken coop, a shed and two rusted cars in the backyard. It was the perfect cliché of a little rez shack. I drove a little farther and the field came into view. Bordered by woods on two sides, it was quiet and no one but us ever seemed to go there anymore.

"We're here!" Charlie announced. He pulled a handgun from the glove compartment. "Smith & Wesson .22 calibre blue steel revolver," he said reverently. We all climbed out of the car. Jasper and Mouse stood on either side of Charlie, looking at the gun in awe.

I shook my head and walked toward the back of the car. I leaned against the trunk, pulling a rolled up bundle of leather out of my pocket. I strapped a bracer on my arm. It had been my Nimosôm's — my mother's father — and I stopped to admire the supple brown leather, worn smooth by years of use. It fit around my arm like it was made for me. I flexed my fingers, limbering them up.

"Whatcha doin', Floyd?" Mouse called. He walked back to where I stood, as I pulled a duffel bag out of the trunk of the beater. "Aren't you going to shoot Charlie's gun?"

"I don't like guns," I answered. The zipper of the bag slid open with a satisfying *SSSSNIIIIK*. I reached in and lifted my bow carefully out of the bag. Mouse's jaw dropped as I reached in again to pull out a leather quiver full of arrows.

"Wow!" he breathed. "Where did you get that?"

I grinned at the awe on his face.

"It was my Nimosôm's," I said, slinging the quiver onto my back.

I had spent hours eyeing the crossbows and compound bows on the Bass Pro Shop website. I had almost bought a new one a

41

couple of times — once I even visited the actual store north of Toronto. But I always ended up changing my mind. My Nimosôm's bow wasn't fancy or expensive. But it carried a history. And its age hadn't stopped me from winning a bunch of trophies with it. I realized it meant more to me than a brand new one ever could.

Nimosôm was a hunter from need rather than for sport. The family ate every animal he killed, and he was a deadly shot with the bow. When everyone else was using rifles, my Nimosôm would say that hunting with a bow and arrow kept him connected to Mother Earth and the animals he hunted. "It's important to keep our culture alive," he'd tell me. "One foot in the past," he'd say. I liked that. I tried to live that way too.

"Come on, Mouse," I said. I handed the bow to him. He held it gently in his hands like it was some kind of treasure. I couldn't help but laugh at the expression on his face.

Jasper was setting up a row of twelve cans on the fence at the back of the field. Charlie was flicking open the cylinder on the .22 and smacking it closed again, then spinning it against the palm of his hand.

"Will you cut that shit out, Charlie!" I growled. I stroked the feather fletchings on an arrow and waited for Jasper to finish setting up.

"It's not loaded, man." Charlie dug a hand into his pocket and pulled out a bunch of bullets. He started loading them into the chambers one by one. I shook my head and notched an arrow onto the bowstring.

When Jasper was finished setting up, he walked back to where we were standing. Charlie finished loading and stepped up, taking position in front of the cans. He held the .22 out in front of him with one hand and turned it sideways. I rolled my eyes. He watched way too many movies about gangs.

CRACK! CRACK! CRACK! The .22 jumped slightly in Charlie's hand as he fired. *CRACK! CRACK!* Charlie tilted his head to the side and looked at the targets. Only two cans had been hit.

"You have three more shots." Jasper smirked.

"I know!" *CRACK! CRACK! CRACK!* Missed. Missed. And missed.

Jasper was doubled over laughing. "My turn!" he said when he could talk again. He grabbed the gun from Charlie and popped open the cylinder. "Charlie, I need more bullets. Mouse, set up a couple more cans! Oh, wait . . . I guess we don't need them." He laughed at his own as Charlie scowled at him.

"NaNaNaaaaa! NaNaNaaaaaa!" Jasper sang as he loaded the gun. Charlie, Mouse, and I watched as he bobbed his head and shuffled his feet.

Charlie tapped him on the shoulder. "What the hell are you singing?"

"*SWAT*, man! I'm a total badass!"

"You're a total *dumb*ass, Jas. That's the theme from *Rocky*."

I fell against Mouse, laughing as Jasper turned confused eyes up at Charlie. Charlie shook his head at him, challenging him to answer back. "Just shoot, man."

Eight quick *CRACKS* and four cans were thrown off the fence.

"Better than you did, Charlie!" Jasper called in response to Charlie's burst of laughter. "I know. Let Mouse have a turn."

"No!" I said so forcefully it was like the word was shot from my mouth. Visions of Aaron danced in my head.

Mouse glanced at over at me, a hurt look on his face. His hand was already held out for the gun.

"I'll go." I smiled at them, trying to make my voice sound softer. "Mouse, you can hold the arrows for me." The smile he gave me was so blindingly bright I could have used sunglasses.

"What do I do?" he asked, holding out a shaking hand for the quiver.

"Just hand me another one right after I shoot, so I don't lose my focus." Mouse nodded and pulled out the first arrow, handing it to me.

I took position and stood with my feet shoulder width apart. I breathed in slowly and pointed my bow downwards, attaching the arrow to the bowstring and holding both with three fingers. Taking a deep breath, I swung the bow up and drew the string back in one fluid motion. I stood like that for a moment. I breathed in the scent of pine from all the trees around us and the smell of the chalk I used on my hands. Then, letting out the breath slowly, I released the string. It made a satisfying *TWANG* and I watched as the arrow sliced through the air. It hit the tin can dead centre and sent it flying.

I held my hand out for another arrow and repeated the motion smoothly. Again, and again . . . arrows flew and cans clattered to the ground. Six shots. There was silence as I lowered my bow and looked at my friends. Mouse was beaming at me and Jasper and Charlie were speechless for once. Charlie looked at the six empty places on the fence.

"Whoa," he breathed. He looked over at Jasper, then at Mouse and finally at me.

"Holy cow, Floyd!" Jasper added.

I smiled at Mouse and patted him on the back. "Thanks, buddy."

Mouse smiled back, his face flushed. It took so little to make Mouse happy. And when Mouse was happy, everyone around him was happy too. I could never understand why anyone would give him a hard time at school. I thought he was pretty cool.

Chapter 8
GRANDPA'S GUN

"Hey, Floyd," Mouse asked, tapping me on the shoulder. "Why don't you like guns? Is it because of Aaron?"

Charlie and Jasper exchanged looks as I looked down at Mouse and tried to smile. I opened my mouth to answer but nothing came out.

"Aaron used a .22," Jasper said. He stared at the gun in his hand.

"Yeah. It was his dad's." Charlie looked grimly at Mouse. "Took it and went out to the woods."

Mouse was looking at them, wide-eyed and tongue-tied.

"It's not because of Aaron," I told him, tousling his hair gently and trying to smile. "It's a long story, Mouse. Just something that happened to me when I was a kid. No big deal." I walked to the car and started to pack up my stuff up.

No big deal. *Right.*

The fact was that my other grandfather — my dad's father — had used guns. Grandpa had taught me how to shoot as soon as I was old enough to hold a gun and keep holding it when it kicked back as I fired it. He took great pride in showing me how to line up the sights and practice shooting cans off the back fence. When I turned out to be a natural crack shot, it was like he had won the lottery or something. He was so proud of my shooting abilities that he would brag to anyone who would listen. He signed me up for local shooting competitions with his handguns. It was the one thing he had always done with me, his version of grandfather/grandson bonding, I suppose. I hadn't been quite as excited by it all as he was. But spending that time with him had been important to me, guns or not.

Grandpa used to drink a lot. And when he was drinking, I tried to avoid him as much as possible. His drinking had rarely spilled over to shooting, luckily. I had loved getting all his attention when he was sober. And making him so proud of me? If there was a better feeling in the world at that point, I didn't know what it was.

That had all been when I was younger than Mouse and I had loved spending time with my grandfather. I liked shooting cans off a wall. I even liked the competitions and I had won my fair share of them.

Over the years, the memory hadn't faded exactly. It had just blurred around the edges a little, like an old picture or a book that had been thumbed through too many times.

But the way it played out still made my blood run cold.

I once read that the best way to get the demons out of your head is to write them down. The worst thing in my head was that experience with my grandfather, so this is what I wrote . . .

The crash of my bedroom door hitting the wall beside my bed as Grandpa threw it open. That's what woke me up that morning. I was being pulled forcibly from a dream about flying to the sound of something banging loudly by my head. I sat up and yelled out in surprise and, quite frankly, terror.

"Floyd! Wake up, boy." Grandpa was smiling strangely and

swaying a little as he closed the door and tossed a package onto my lap. I peered at him through sleep-blurred eyes, mouth open and chest heaving as I tried to catch my breath. I had never liked being startled awake. And Grandpa's sudden, crashing entry was almost more than I could safely take without a mini heart attack.

"Don't just look at me, silly! Open it!" He belched into his fist.

I rubbed a hand across my eyes and looked at him. He had been drinking. And it must have been pretty heavily. I could tell from the way he was hanging on to the end of my bed to hold himself upright. I glanced at the long package in front of me. It wasn't my birthday and it wasn't Christmas. I touched the plain brown paper cautiously.

I tore the paper off in long strips. SNIIIICK. SNIIIICK. I read the words written on the box in my lap. Remington Model Seven Youth Rifle.

"Thanks, Grandpa. We'll have to do some target practice sometime." I yawned widely and lay back down, pulling the blanket around my shoulders.

I tried to close my eyes and go back to sleep but he reached past me to pull the gun out of its box. He held it up to point out its finer features.

"Look at this workmanship!" He was clearly proud of his purchase. He breathed his boozy breath in my direction.

"This is the best rifle on the market for a beginning hunter! Centre-fire, bolt action, adjustable rifle sights, sling swivel studs, and a hinged floor-plate magazine . . . it's a beauty, isn't it?"

What did he say? Sling swivel studs? What did that even mean?

"I even had a sight put on it, just like mine." He fumbled with a bunch of shells he had pulled out of his pocket. He tried to load them into the rifle.

"Grandpa, maybe you shouldn't load it right now." I was sitting up, suddenly wide awake.

"Ssfine," he muttered at me. He pushed my hands away when I tried to reach for the gun. "I can do it!" he shouted. But the bullets tumbled from his shaking hands and rolled onto the floor. "Dammit!" He tried to crawl under the bed to gather them.

"Grandpa! Just leave them, please!" I looked around the room, desperately. How were my parents sleeping through all the noise he was making?

Grandpa finally got his hand on a bullet and loaded it into the rifle. "There!"

He swung the rifle around the room until the barrel was pointing right at me. I threw my hands in the air stupidly.

The gun was loaded. He was drunk. I saw his finger trembling. I could see it tightening slightly, starting to put pressure on the trigger.

They say that your life flashes before your eyes when you're about to die. I was one hundred percent positive I was about to be accidentally shot in the head by my drunken grandfather. But I didn't see anything except that endless rifle barrel pointed at my face.

"Grandpa. Please put the gun down."

He looked blearily at me. Then understanding suddenly dawned on him. His mouth dropped open as a look of horror crossed his face.

He lowered the gun and reached for me. I recoiled against my headboard, my heart still pounding.

"Floyd," he whispered. "Oh, god. I'm sorry, son. I didn't mean . . . I wouldn't have . . ."

I don't know all the reasons for what happened next. But even then I knew that Grandpa being drunk was part of it. I still had my hand out, waiting for him to hand me the gun. He leaned toward me let me take it from him. I unloaded it and held the shell in my shaking hand. I turned to say something, anything to defuse the situation. And Grandpa was pulling a handgun from under the tail of his shirt.

"Whoa!" I put my hands up again. Another gun?
Why would he be carrying that? "Grandpa, what are
you doing?"

Grandpa wasn't pointing the gun at me. He raised it in his
trembling hand, tears running down his face. He held it
under his own chin.

"Grandpa, stop!"

"All I do is mess things up. I'm sorry, Floyd." His finger
tightened. I saw the trigger move slightly.

"Stop! Grandpa, it's okay." Where was my dad? "Dad!"

"You'd all be better off without me."

Grandpa was sobbing. But he still held the gun tightly
against his throat.

"No . . . no." I was shaking my head, sobbing along with
him. I reached toward him. "Don't!"

The door flew open and my father burst in. His large
frame took up the doorway and blocked my mother
who was a step behind him. He took in what was
happening. His father crying and holding a gun under
his chin. His terrified son kneeling behind the old man on
the bed, begging him to give him the gun.

"Floyd, go with your mom," Dad said calmly.

"D-Dad?" I hiccupped, unable to move.

"Cardinal, take him outside — quickly." He was talking to
my mom, but his eyes never left mine. He moved into the
room and gave me a nod and traded places with me on
the bed. As I walked out with my mother hugging me close
against her, I heard Dad murmuring gently to his father.
I looked back to see him sliding an arm around Grandpa's
heaving shoulders.

My mom took me to my aunt's house for the rest of the night.
Grandpa lived to see another day. But those days were short.
He took his life fifteen months later with the rifle he had
given me that night.

Chapter 9
CHIEF

I let Charlie drive back. Mouse had to get home and Charlie was a more aggressive driver than I was. I tended to stick to the speed limit, even on the rez. But Charlie drove like he had a horde of flesh-eating zombies chasing him. I didn't want Mouse to be late and suffer the wrath of his mother, Raynetta. She was actually pretty great but her big pet peeve was her family being late to meals. So Charlie was driving.

We got there in record time. I hopped out of the car with Mouse. Jasper and Charlie wanted to cruise around the rez and offer rides to any of the girls out walking. I felt like walking myself, and maybe checking on my mom at the community centre.

"Don't drive it into the ground," I told them, closing the passenger door carefully behind me.

"Too late!" Jasper yelled over the roar of the engine as they peeled away from Mouse's house, laughing.

"Want to come in for a bit?" Mouse asked. Hope was written all over his face.

I hated to disappoint him but remembering Grandpa had me thinking about Aaron again. I really wanted to try to talk to my dad about what could be done. But I needed my mom's advice first. Dad didn't want to hear what I had to say and I knew Mom could help me figure out how to make him listen.

"Sorry, buddy. I need to go talk to my mom."

He didn't say a word, but his face kind of crumpled. I hated that I had done that, taken away his contagious smile.

"We'll do something soon, okay? Promise."

There was the smile again, like the sun rising. "Okay!" He grinned. He leaped up the stairs to his front door.

I watched Mouse scurry into the house. I knew he was bullied at school. He was way smaller than the other kids his age. And he was more sensitive than most. When he got to high school, I would be able look out for him. But I couldn't stop what was happening every time he left home for middle school. I wished I could.

I had endured the usual ribbing and the odd snide remark like anyone else when I was Mouse's age. But there were a couple of townies who had had a problem with anyone from the rez. They took great pleasure in shoving me into lockers and knocking my books out of my hands. It had escalated to name calling — things like Squaw or Pocahontas, which I assumed was because of my long hair. I put up with a lot back then. At least until I hit puberty and shot up six inches. Once I started shoving back, they moved on to easier targets.

Like Mouse.

And I knew it wasn't just the kids who could be idiots. When I was younger, I had had to sit through a class as a substitute teacher ranted about how people on the reserve should get off their asses and stop living off taxpayers. How he was sick of paying for a bunch of "lazy Indians" to sit around the rez and drink away their government income. Charlie and Jasper had been in the same class. I had watched Charlie get redder and redder in the face as the teacher went on and on. Jasper's hands made such tight fists he ended up with fingernail cuts on his palms. I told my parents and we never had that teacher again. My mom saw to that.

I headed for the community centre, saying hello to friends and neighbours as I walked past. I knew everyone in the community was thinking about the girls who had died and the one who was still alive. I knew they were remembering the other kids we'd lost to suicide over the last year. I hoped a few were still thinking about Aaron. I missed him so much in that moment, it actually hurt.

The community centre was an old building that sat in the middle of the rez like a watchtower. I'd heard my mom talk about the plans they had for it when it was built. But the money never came through, and it never became what it was supposed to be. We all knew it was there but no one except the elders used it. They'd gather to play cards or gossip. We didn't have a church, so services were held there on Sundays. Sometimes there were potluck dinners there. But there weren't any formal programs or professional help. Kids tended to steer clear. It had turned into a spot for their grandparents, not for themselves.

I had always thought that the centre could have been a haven for the kids on the rez. It should have been a safe place to go when things got loud or tough at home. A place to learn new skills or share traditional ones. A place to get counselling or learn more about colleges or universities. Maybe tutoring. Definitely sports. A place that would help us see that we had something to offer and a future ahead of us.

I swung the door open and stepped inside. It was quiet. With the suicides last night, I thought no one would be there. The women would be with Theresa, trying to comfort her and bringing her food. But it turns out my mother was getting things ready for them to meet there later. They would drink tea and talk or whatever the women did when they got together.

I heard my mom's voice before I saw her. She was in one of the back rooms. And she was loud. I stopped dead. I had rarely heard her using anything but her usual soft and respectful voice. But she was shouting — either in anger or frustration.

"You're the chief, Victor!" she yelled. "It's up to you to do something!" She was talking to my dad! I had *never* heard her raise her voice to my dad in my entire life.

"These kids need something to live for!" she went on. "We need a real counsellor for them to talk to. We need resources and jobs. We need to show them what they have to contribute to our community and the world. We need to show them where they come from and where they could go. We need to show them that they have a future. We can't continue like this, Victor! Our community is dying!"

"Cardinal," my father tried to break into my mom's rant. But even from out in the hallway, I could tell she wasn't finished yet.

"Our son is hereditary chief, Victor. He has the knowledge, but it's time for him to share it. He needs to start learning from you how to preserve our culture and pass on our traditions. And you can learn from him. Listen to him! Let him help! He knows what the kids need more than we do."

I had come to ask my mom's advice, and found her doing what I hadn't had the nerve to do myself. I should have said exactly what she was saying. I knew I could help somehow. But it became clear that I needed a plan. If I was hereditary chief, I should be standing up for our people. I should be supporting and helping them. Now was my chance. I could go in and, very calmly, ask my dad to listen to what I had to say. Maybe with my mom's support, he'd finally let me help. I took a step toward the room.

Then I heard my father's voice. "He's a child, Cardinal. He has no idea what this community needs. Neither do you. I'm the Chief! I will *not* have my wife yelling at me like a harpy! Let me do my job!"

"Which job, Victor? You've taken on too much. You should have stuck to being hereditary chief and found ways to pass on what you know. Why wasn't that enough? Now you're chief councilor too? It's too much for you. It would be too much for anyone. We're falling apart."

"I know that! But Floyd is too young to take any of this on! Let it go!"

I stepped back. It was clear Dad wasn't going to listen to me. Not now. Not if he wouldn't even listen to my mother.

I couldn't imagine the stress he must be under. But I also couldn't understand why he wouldn't let anyone try to help. I left as quietly as I could.

~~Dear Diary~~

Someday I'll figure out how to start these things without sounding like a thirteen-year-old girl.

I'm still trying to wrap my head around the idea of my mom confronting my dad like that. I can't believe he said those things about me. I really can't believe he yelled at my mom. My parents never fight and I've never heard him talk to her like that. Just for a second, he sounded like he hated both of us.

That's stupid. I know it is. My dad loves us. But I think what's going on here — all the people we've lost — is weighing pretty heavily on him. He's lashing out. I want to cut him some slack. But I want to help and he's shutting me out.

If I ever have a son, I'll listen to him.

Even if I'm falling apart at the seams.

Chapter 10
THE GUYS

I wandered down the road, listening for the sound of the beater. I needed to hear what my friends thought before I made any more plans to waylay my father.

I knew how to find one of my friends, at least. I swung back around toward Mouse's place. I'd seen the kid eat and figured he had probably had more than enough time to finish lunch. Sure enough, he was sitting on the old swing hanging from the maple tree in his front yard. He was frowning down at a notebook in his lap. He erased something and gently blew away the eraser dust before leaning down and sketching something onto the paper.

"What are you working on?" I asked.

Mouse jumped and almost fell off the swing. He quickly closed the sketchpad. "Nothing," he said, pushing his hair out of his eyes and leaving a smudge of lead on his forehead.

"You've got a little something there." I pointed toward the spot on his face. He rubbed at it. Now he had a bigger smudge.

"I'll get it," I laughed. I pulled a tissue out of my pocket and cleaned him up.

"Thanks, Floyd." He smiled up at me. "Hey, what are you doing here?"

"I need to talk to the guys about something. I thought I'd see if you wanted to come."

"Me?" He looked completely shocked. "Why?"

"You're one of the guys too, right?" I asked him.

His face lit up. "Well . . . yeah. I guess so." His chest puffed with pride as he leaped off the swing. "Let me just put this stuff inside and tell my mom." He was running toward the house before I could answer.

I wondered how well Mouse knew the girls with the suicide pact. I wondered if they had been bullied like he was. He didn't like to talk about it, but I had heard his mom talking to mine. Mouse had come home crying a few times and with bruises a couple of others. Maybe I could teach him how to throw a punch or something so the kids at his school would stop bothering him. I had tried talking to him but he clammed up as soon as I mentioned it. If I ever caught those kids, they'd better run a lot faster than me or they'll be the ones going home with bruises.

We found the beater before we found the guys. They had left it parked at the side of the road. Mouse spun around in a slow circle.

"Where are they?" he asked. There really weren't very many places they could have gone. They had left the car at the edge of a field.

"I have no idea," I told him. We settled down on the ground beside the car to wait. They had to come back at some point, I figured.

I settled back against the tire well of the beater and stuck a piece of grass in my mouth. With no idea when the guys would be back, I figured we at least had time for a story. "So, Mouse, did I ever tell you about the time some kids at school teased me about my braids?"

"No. They teased you?" Mouse frowned and touched his own braid.

"Yeah, man! There were a whole bunch of them. Started pushing me around and pulling my hair. They said I looked like a girl."

"You don't look like a girl!"

"I know! I look like a freakin' warrior with this hair!"

"I've got long hair." Mouse smiled.

"'Cause you're a warrior too, man!"

"You think so?"

"For sure. For us, long hair is about spirituality and power, Mouse. Anyone who makes fun of your hair is an idiot who doesn't know anything about us or our culture."

Mouse smiled. "So what did you do to those boys?" he asked eagerly. "Did you beat them up?"

"Nah. They weren't worth it. It takes a stronger man to walk away sometimes. But I did tell them why I wore my hair long. Figured maybe if they understood, they'd leave me alone."

"Did they?"

"Of course not," I told him. My voice was light, but I knew Mouse was hanging on my every word. "Bullies get off on bullying people."

"So then what did you do?" he asked breathlessly.

"I focused on the biggest bully. I told him if he didn't back off and take his buddies with him, he'd wake up one day and find himself shaved bald. I told him that on the rez they teach us how to scalp people when we're young."

Mouse doubled over laughing. "I bet he stopped bullying you when you said that," he giggled.

"Wouldn't you?" I asked him.

"Yeah," he said. Then he looked thoughtful. "Do you think that would work for me?"

"Are they still bothering you at school?" I asked.

But Mouse didn't get a chance to answer.

"Jeez, we leave the car alone for fifteen minutes and a couple of thugs take it over," Jasper's voice called out from behind us. He was trudging toward us with Charlie, who was carrying a red fuel container.

"What happened?" I asked. I was pretty sure I already knew the answer.

"Ran out of gas," Charlie hollered. "Had to walk to the station."

"You didn't notice the gauge was low?" I asked. "Nah, it wasn't. It's stuck again," Jasper said, dropping down on the ground beside us. "I'll take it apart later and try to fix it."

"What are you guys doing here?" Charlie asked. He was filling the tank carefully.

"I needed to talk to all of you." I spit the blade of grass out of my mouth and wiped my hands on my jeans. "So I overhead my parents talking after we dropped off Mouse. My mom was yelling." The guys looked surprised at this. I didn't blame them. "I know. She never yells. But she was yelling and saying that our community is dying and that something has to be done about it. My mom thinks I should help somehow. I've been trying to come up with some ideas but my dad doesn't want to talk about it. He thinks I'm just a kid."

My friends were watching me intently. I wished my father would listen as avidly as they did. It struck me that I was lucky to have these guys. They would listen to whatever I had to say. And I knew that if there was anything they could do to help, they would, without question. Something about having their attention got me thinking about the possibilities of what we could make happen. About what we could really do to help if we did it together. My dad didn't want to listen to me but there was no way he could ignore all of us.

So I kept going with it. "Kids . . . our friends . . . are killing themselves because they can't see a future. They don't see that there's a life for them here . . . that they can do something with their lives if they stay. Or that they can leave if they really want to. We just lost four girls. We've been losing other kids steadily. We lost one of our best friends."

I felt tears sting my eyes and I swallowed hard. Mouse patted my back, a tear sliding down his cheek. He had loved Aaron as much as any of us. I gave him a small smile before continuing.

"There's got to be something we can do to show other kids that we have a future. On the rez or out there." I gestured vaguely down the road, away from everything that was familiar to us.

"Do we though?" Charlie asked. "Because there's not much here for us. And there's nothing for us out there. Where the hell are we supposed to go? Nowhere. Zero future, man."

"We have futures, Charlie," Jasper disagreed. "We just have no idea what they are."

"I don't know," Charlie continued. "You know my cousin William?" When we all nodded, he went on. "He went to the city after high school. Lasted a few months and then came back home. He said people were awful there. He couldn't get a job. He applied everywhere but people took one look at him and said the job was already taken. People were racist to him. Like, *really* racist. He got into some kind of fight with a kid who called him a savage. The kid got his friends together and they jumped William and beat him up pretty badly. William OD'd after that. Took the bottle of painkillers he got at the hospital and downed all of it. They had to pump his stomach. His parents brought him home and told everyone he had gotten into an accident. They swore the whole family to secrecy about the overdose."

"I . . . I don't know what to say," I told him. "I'm sorry, man."

Charlie shrugged.

"But it's not like that for everyone, right?" Jasper asked. "People leave and do okay."

"Like who?" Charlie asked.

"My sister," Mouse piped up. "She's doing great at her school!"

"Yeah. I guess," Charlie said.

"Have you ever thought about it?" I asked. "What you'll do after high school?"

Jasper shrugged. "I don't know. I guess. Sometimes."

"Have you guys ever thought of leaving the rez? Maybe going to university?"

Charlie shook his head. "I'd never get in. I don't have the marks."

Jasper nodded at that. "Yeah, I don't know. No one has ever really talked about it with me. At school, the guidance counsellor said I could do a mechanics course or something. But no one ever asked about university. I don't know what I'd study anyway," he admitted.

"I always kind of wanted to go," I told them. "I thought maybe I could be a teacher or something."

My friends looked at me in complete shock. I had never talked to them about what I wanted to do after high school. I had kind of been afraid to admit it to myself. But I thought maybe I could be the kind of teacher who inspired kids to be more than they ever imagined they could be. I had watched that old movie, *Dead Poets Society*, with my mom and wished I had a teacher like that. That's the kind of teacher I'd be. Maybe I could write books at night and teach kids during the day. That sounded pretty much perfect to me.

Maybe I *could* teach. Maybe my storytelling could go beyond shooting the shit with my friends and writing in my diary. Journal. Whatever. I wasn't ready to admit that to my friends though. The whole teacher thing was enough for now.

"I think you'd make a great teacher, Floyd," Mouse told me.

"Thanks, buddy." I focused on him. "What about you? What do you think you'll do after school?"

He ducked his head shyly. "I don't know. I'd really like to be an artist. I think I could make really good comic books. I want to create a Native superhero who would rescue kids like us, who would save the world! But I could do that anywhere." He tugged self-consciously at his braid. "If I did leave . . . I think I'd like to go to art school."

We were all gaping at him. I knew Mouse liked to draw. But I had no idea how big his dreams actually were.

"A Native superhero, eh? I'd love to see some of your art," I said. I watched as his entire face lit up.

"Really, Floyd?"

"Yeah, me too," Jasper added. "You should make him look like me." He struck a pose and smiled at Mouse.

Charlie slapped Mouse on the back and grinned widely. "You definitely have to show us, man. I wish I could draw!"

It sounds corny, but I really loved my friends at that moment.

"Well . . . maybe I could teach you," Mouse suggested.

Charlie nodded. "What I'd really like to see is a story about —" and Charlie dove into an animated conversation with Mouse. He talked about his favourite comic books and superheroes and the Native twist he thought Mouse could put on them.

I watched Mouse talk, his face open and excited. All of a sudden, he was so confident. He was listening to Charlie and telling him about his own ideas for his comic books. There was no sign of the bullied kid when he talked about art and comics. I vowed then to do everything in my power to support this kid so I could see him come alive like this all the time. If we could bring that out in Mouse, maybe we could find a way to do the same for the other kids on the rez.

Chapter 11
TRADITION

I use my writing to vent and to work out different things that are floating around in my head. When I'm upset, I write angry poetry and horror stories à la Stephen King. When I'm happy, I write funny stuff — short stories or quirky haiku poems. And when I'm sad, I write depressing stories about loss and heartache. If I can write out my feelings and actually create something that makes me feel better . . . then maybe other kids could too. Not necessarily just with words. But maybe they could draw like Mouse, or paint or sing. Or maybe they could do something more traditional, like beadwork or wood carving. Maybe some of them worked out their emotions by kicking a ball around.

It was the start of what I thought was a really great idea. And the more I thought about it, the more I liked it.

Art didn't have to be just a way for kids to work out their emotions or whatever. It could also be a way to connect all of us with our culture. We needed to find ways to stay alive as a community. Maybe it would help us find our way back to what we were in the first place: speaking our languages, creating our art, and writing our stories.

We needed to remember where we came from.

But it wasn't just about creating art or stories. It was about making a life for ourselves that celebrates our history. What about sports? What about hunting? We needed to be turning our guns on something other than pop cans and ourselves. If we used our traditions to communicate and work out what we were feeling, maybe we wouldn't be so quick to self-destruct.

×　×　×

"Soccer and lacrosse would be awesome!" Charlie crowed. "We could start a team. Give those townies a run for their money."

"We could make money?" Jasper asked. "Like gambling?"

"It's a figure of speech, Jas. Although . . . a couple of bucks on a game here and there . . . you never know."

"I like the idea of art classes," Mouse volunteered. "Maybe we could have a cartooning class. Or comic book art." His ears were turning a little pink — like he was embarrassed to be suggesting it.

"Yeah!" I said, wanting to keep him involved. "Maybe you could teach it, Mouse."

"Me? Really?"

"We're all going to need to pitch in. You guys can coach sports teams," I told Jasper and Charlie.

"And you could teach writing," Mouse said.

I nodded. This could work. We could really bring our friends together and try to keep them safe.

We ended up staying out and talking a lot longer than I meant to. I missed dinner, but had sent my mom a quick text to let her know. So I knew I wasn't going to be in trouble or anything. She'd have gone to bed already but I knew she'd have left a plate for me to heat up.

The walk across the rez was quieter than usual. On a summer night, there were usually people sitting outside their houses on lawn chairs, gossiping and having a drink. Some of the kids would still be up, running around and screaming while their mothers yelled that it was way past their bedtime. But it had gotten pretty sombre around here lately. I knew that news of the suicide pact had gotten around. Parents were holding onto their kids a little tighter tonight. I was anxious to get home and talk to my dad about the ideas the guys and I had come up with.

I looked up and noticed that I was walking past Aaron's place. I hadn't been inside since he died. But I had spent half my childhood at that house. It was as familiar to me as my own home. I stopped out front without even thinking.

I still missed Aaron every single day. I had known he was unhappy. He had taken a lot of crap from the kids at school and even from some of the boys on the rez. He had told me he was gay a few years ago. I was cool with it. I had pretty much known since he was a little kid anyway. As far as I was concerned, it didn't change anything between us. He was still the same guy to me. But not everyone felt that way about him. Particularly his father. Aaron had taken a beating from his dad that left him bruised for a week after he came out to his family. But I had thought he was doing okay. I really had.

Then I had received a call from his mom, asking if he was with me.

He wasn't.

I stared at the front door. I remembered heading over that morning and talking to Aaron's mom, hearing how he hadn't come home the night before. I remember telling her that he was probably just hanging out in the woods. He used to do that, especially when his dad was on his case. I had gone out to check the places I knew he hung out when he needed to get away. I never thought for a second that anything was wrong.

Not until I had found him by the river. He had still been holding the gun he had used to kill himself.

I took one last look at Aaron's house and started walking, faster and faster. I was trying to outrun the cloud of grief that threatened to take over again.

I had tried to write about Aaron after he died. But every time I picked up a pen, I'd just stare at my notebook and see his face; the blood and leaves in his hair. I had no words that could erase that picture. No story could change that.

Until I finally sat down and forced myself to write a letter to him. I didn't need to look in my notebook to remember it. Every word was etched into my brain.

Dear Aaron,

I wish I had written this a week ago. Two weeks ago. A year ago. I wish I had just talked to you. Just listened better. Asked more questions. Told you that it doesn't matter who you want to have sex with. You're still my best friend.

I still can't believe that you're gone. You've been gone for a week. But it still feels like you're going to climb in my window and crash on my floor, eating Oreos, and talking late into the night.

I still walk past your house and expect to see you sitting on the porch, waiting for me. Or I hear my phone and expect it to be a text from you.

Even though I know that you're gone.

Because I'm the one who found you. Found you lying on the ground with a gun in your hand. I still see you lying there every single time I close my eyes.

I hate you for that.

But I miss you way more than I could ever hate you.

I loved you like a brother, Aaron.

Still love you.

Even now.

Always.

I wish I had told you that.

I wish I could have saved you.

Your friend forever,
Floyd

I didn't mind walking in the dark. I had lived here all my life. There wasn't anywhere I wasn't comfortable and there was no corner I wasn't familiar with. But it just didn't feel the same since Aaron died.

Our house was dark when I got home. My parents had been going to bed early lately. I knew they were under a lot of stress. So was everyone else. That accounted for the eerie quiet on a warm summer night.

I didn't really have a curfew in the summer. But with everything that was going on . . . my mom liked me home at a decent hour. I didn't want to wake her or my dad up and since the front door squeaked like crazy, I went around the back. I unlocked the door *super* quietly and tiptoed into the kitchen.

Made it.

As I made my way carefully toward my bedroom, I heard a sound coming out of the living room. I stopped in the doorway and peered into the darkness. I could make out the outline of my father sitting in his favourite chair, facing the front window. I was going to step into the room but a sound stopped me cold. It was my father's sobbing. I had never heard my father cry before. I was sure he wouldn't want anyone to hear him now. I took a step back and turned toward my room. I moved silently away from my father and left him alone with his grief.

Chapter 12
BIG PLANS

I walked into the kitchen the next morning. I wasn't entirely sure what I was going to find. Would my dad still be sitting in the living room, crying? Would my mom be with him? Would one of them — or both — be yelling? Probably not, since I would have heard them from my room. Maybe they were finally talking. Maybe he'd finally listen to me.

My father was sitting at the table. He was smiling widely and talking to my mom. There was absolutely no sign of the distraught man from last night. Unless you looked closely. He may have had a smile on his face but it didn't reach his eyes.

"I really think we're on the right track here," he was saying. "The Council and I have something big planned. I think it'll really make a difference."

"What will?" I asked. I sat down across from him and studied his face. He somehow managed to look like he had slept for twelve hours.

"I can't tell you yet, Floyd," he said, sipping his coffee. "We have a few more loose ends to tie up first. But I think it'll really do some good."

"Ummm . . . that's . . . good." I had no idea what he had planned. But anything that would help the community had my support. "Let me know if there's anything I can do."

"Sure. Sure. I'm off to meet the Council now. We're going to make some big decisions today." He stood up and grabbed my mom. He spun her around, dishwater flying as he dipped her and went in for a kiss. He left in a cloud of optimism that didn't seem entirely real.

"So . . . he's in a good mood," I said to my mom.

She nodded and sat down beside me, wiping her hands on a dishtowel. "Yes. I guess he thinks the Council is going to start fixing some of our problems."

"Do you think they will?"

My mom sighed heavily, looking troubled. "I don't know, Floyd. I hope so. We can't just ignore what's going on. We've had twenty-four suicide attempts in the past couple of months."

"*What*? No. No way. That can't be right."

"It is," my mom insisted.

I felt like I was going to pass out. *That* many people had tried to kill themselves? That couldn't be true. How could it be? Wouldn't someone have come in and done something? Wouldn't we be on the news?

"No. That's impossible." I felt like I had been punched in the stomach. There was just no way it could be right.

"I know. But it's true."

"Why aren't we on the news? I mean . . . why isn't anyone doing anything to help us?" I'm not sure who I thought could swoop in and rescue us. But twenty-four suicide attempts in just a few weeks sounded like a national crisis to me!

"I don't know, Floyd. Your father tried to get the media to pay attention. But they had just covered suicide among young people on another reserve. They told him that the story had already been done."

"'Already been done'?" I nearly gagged. I just couldn't wrap my head around it. "Did they do anything to help the other reserve?" I asked.

My mom shook her head. "No. Nothing."

"And that was it?" I demanded. "They did the story and then just left without trying to help them?"

My mom sighed. "They also did a follow-up story."

"About what?"

"After the news story aired, there was an increase in the number of suicide attempts on that reserve."

"An increase? Why?"

"Something about suicide being contagious."

"Contagious how?" I asked. This was so mind-blowing.

"They said that seeing stories on the news about suicide can give people the idea that it's a way out for them too."

"Then why would they do another story?"

She sighed and rubbed at her temples. I didn't blame her. My own head was ready to combust thanks to all the new information hitting it. "I don't know, Maskosis. I don't understand any of this either."

"But how could it be twenty-four? Here on *this* reserve?"

"I really don't know, son. But more people are trying. Not just kids either. We've been trying to keep it from most people, but Mr. Fortier's death a couple of weeks ago was a suicide. Some don't really want to die. Some do and don't succeed. Some try more than once."

"That's awful."

"It is."

"But still . . . twenty-four. That's a lot."

"Yes. Too many." She took my hand and stroked it. I hadn't realized so many people had wanted to die enough to actually try killing themselves. Or that they would try more than once if they failed. I wondered briefly if Aaron had tried before he succeeded.

"Someone needs to do something," I said. I thought of all of the ideas the guys and I had talked about.

"I know you want to help, Floyd. You care so much. For our people and our home. That's what will make you a great Chief someday."

I thought about my mother's words as I headed to my room. I had to meet my friends soon but first I needed to write. It was the only thing I could do to try and get my head around all of this. I don't know why I was shocked that it wasn't just young people who were looking for a way out. What kind of future did the rez have if there weren't any kids my age and younger left?

Would I make a good Chief? Not if I didn't start standing up to my dad and talk to him about my ideas. I vowed to myself to find a way to make him listen.

Lights up.

All is quiet on the rez.

The smells of fry bread, dry leaves, and dying fires permeate the autumn air.

Old Mr. Fortier rocks on his front porch, looking down at a well-worn photo album.

His wedding album.

Photos of his wife, who he lost.

Mr. Fortier: So beautiful.

He runs his fingers over a photo of his wife, beaming on their wedding day.

Mr. Fortier: I never thought you'd be the one to leave. I figured I'd be the first to go. I knew you'd be sad. But you'd carry on with your church group and your flower garden. Your friends would come around and visit every day. Their husbands would come and help take care of the house and the yard after I was gone. You'd be fine. Maybe you'd even get married again. But me? I don't know what to do without you.

He turns one page, then another. He sighs.

Mr. Fortier: I've tried. I really have. I lie awake in our bed and try to ignore the cold, empty spot beside me where you used to dream. I sit at our table and try not to look at the empty chair across from me. I wake up. I go to bed. And I try not to feel like I'm completely alone.

He closes the photo album and picks up a handgun, running his fingers over the cold metal the same way he caressed the photos of his wife.

Mr. Fortier: I miss you. Every single minute I'm here without you is painful. I could live without you . . . sadly. Unhappily. Desperately. Without any hope. My life is as empty as this house is without you. So I choose this.

He holds up the gun.

Mr. Fortier: Because this is easier than trying to live this life here.

Lights go down until we are left in complete darkness.

The silence is broken by the cracking sound of a gunshot.

Chapter 13
SELLING OUR PAST

It was a perfect day for walking. A light breeze kept the late August heat from settling too heavily. The soft sounds of the rez were comforting, even though I could hear everything I'd eaten for breakfast churning around in my stomach. I had no idea what my father was up to. But I knew that the ideas I had were good ones and worth my dad's time to listen to.

I picked the guys up on my way past. I didn't really have a destination in mind. I just needed my friends with me. Or at least I thought I did. Then Charlie and Jasper started one of their crazy debates.

They kept pace beside me, step for step. They were chattering like a couple of blackbirds. The sound of their voices was raucous and grated in my ears as I tried to tune them out. It didn't work.

"Venom is just another side of Spider-Man, right?" Charlie's voice cut into my thoughts. *Here we go again.* This had been an ongoing argument since we'd binge-watched a bunch of superhero movies a few weeks ago. You should have heard them after we saw *The Incredible Hulk*. Charlie was completely obsessed with the fact that Bruce Banner's shirts always got ripped to shreds when he hulked out, but not his pants. It was enough to make you want to drive a stick through your eardrum, just so you could avoid listening to them go on and on.

"Nah, man. Venom is some kind of alien life form who attacks Spider-Man. Everyone knows that."

"I'm telling you, Jas . . . it's the same guy!"

"Did you even see the freakin' movie, man? Wasn't that you sitting right beside me? If Venom was Spider-Man, how the hell did he end up on that other guy, *fighting* Spider-Man? He wasn't fighting himself, man!"

"Maybe! Maybe it was one of those good versus evil things, Jas! One of those, whatdoyoucallits? When something makes no sense?"

"An enigma, like E. Nygma, the Riddler," I muttered. They even had me doing it! "For crying out loud, can you two stop arguing about this crap? Charlie, it's not the same freakin' guy, okay? Jeez."

There was silence for almost a minute.

"I told you so." Jasper always needed to have the last word. I caught his furtive glance in my direction and rolled my eyes. "Anyway, what are we doing today? Charlie's staying at my place tonight. You want to stay too, Floyd? My mom's working so we have the place to ourselves."

It was tempting. Pizza and a movie, maybe some PS4. "Yeah, maybe. We should invite Mouse too," I said.

"But . . . then we can't watch *Deadpool*! It's restricted. He's too young for that movie. I don't want any part in corrupting our youth, man," Jasper said, folding his arms across his chest. I stared at him, trying to decide if he was being serious.

He was.

I caught Charlie's eye and we both burst out laughing.

"What?" Jasper asked. "He's just a little kid!"

We were gasping for air at this point.

"Stop!" Charlie gasped, holding his stomach. "You're killing me, man!"

"Oh, shut up." Jasper pushed Charlie, sending him crashing to the ground. It didn't help. Charlie was still laughing from where he lay.

"Hey, what are those?" I asked, nodding toward some fluttering neon-coloured papers. They seemed to be attached to everything we passed. One blew past me. Charlie reached over and grabbed it. He frowned at it as he got to his feet.

"What's it say?" Jasper demanded, trying to look over Charlie's shoulder. Charlie elbowed him away. "Charlie! Let me see! Come on!"

Jasper snatched at the paper but Charlie held it above his head. I reached over and took it from him.

I read silently. It was something about an appearance by "film star Kevin Feldman" at the community centre. *Oh, jeez.* What the hell was my dad thinking? Was this his big plan? I crumpled it up and stuffed it in my pocket before the guys could read it.

"What does it say, Floyd?" Jasper asked.

"Nothing. It's garbage. Come on. Let's go down to the lake."

Me and my friends spent most summer days down by the lake. Teenagers were drawn there like ants to honey. Usually someone brought a bottle of cheap whiskey to pass around. Relationships started on the shores of the lake. Couples were just as likely to end things there as well. Fights broke out and accusations flew back and forth. He cheated. She cheated. He got into too many fist fights. She spent too much time gossiping with her friends. He was a selfish asshole. She was a stuck-up bitch. There was always something to do or someone to watch down at the lake. The lake was better than TV to me and my friends.

It was also a good place to escape from home when things got too crazy. I had been going down there for years to find a place to be by myself. At sunset, the loons came out and put on a show, calling to each other and gliding back and forth on the water right in front of the shore. There was a spot down the beach from the bonfire pit where I could sit back against an old log by myself and just think. I thought about escaping a lot when I was younger — taking off and moving far, far away. But I had never known any home other than the rez and this was where my heart was. The forest, the lake, the houses, and the people . . . they were a part of me. It was hard to explain. But this place was in my blood.

The guys and I walked down toward the water. I was thinking of my dad and his "grand plan" with Kevin Feldman. The guys were embroiled in yet another superhero debate. Jasper was bouncing around Charlie excitedly.

"Dude! Dude! Listen. So if, like, Batman and Superman got into a fight, who do you think would win? Not like that lame movie. Like in real life."

Oh, for crying out loud. Not this crap again.

I raised my hand to get their attention but Jasper was on a roll.

"'Cause Superman can fly and he's super strong, right? But Batman has the freakin' Batmobile, man! He's got that Bat Grappler hook thing! He's got Batarangs!"

I didn't know whether to laugh or cry as I watched Charlie shove him away.

"Jasper, will you shut up, man? What is this psychotic obsession with superheroes? Superman is the freakin' Man of Steel, ya dick! How the hell is a Batarang supposed to stop Superman?"

So much for thinking Charlie might be the voice of reason. And there was another of those stupid flyers! Jasper grabbed one before I could distract him. His eyes darted across the page, widening slightly.

"Hey! You guys seen this?" Jasper held out the crumpled flyer. Charlie reached out took it from him. He scowled as he read it. I already knew what it said.

NATIVE YOUTH FOR A BETTER TOMORROW!

Come out and see how you can make a difference in your community!

Saturday night – 7:00 p.m.

with special guest speaker, film star Kevin Feldman

"Some meeting of the elders trying to warn us about the dangers of booze, drugs, and sex?" Jasper laughed.

"Not like we're getting much of *any* of that stuff." Charlie rolled his eyes skyward. "Why are they bringing in Kevin Feldman to talk to us? I mean, what the hell would *he* know about native youth?"

"What do you mean?" Jasper asked.

"He's a white guy, man! What the hell do they think a white guy is going to have to say? Does he live on a rez? No. Has he spent time on a rez? No. Does he actually *know* anyone who lives on a rez? No!"

"Maybe he saw one in a movie once," Jasper shot back.

"It's one thing for the elders to have something to say about our lives. But some white actor who happened to ride a horse in one movie? Because he spent some time with a bunch of Indians who were the extras on his lame-ass movie, he thinks he knows anything about us? I hate that crap, man! What a dick!"

I laughed. I couldn't help it. Kevin Feldman *was* a dick. He was a no talent Hollywood hack. My dad actually liked his movies — his *early* movies — from when he was a kid. I guess they were okay. Mostly because of the other kids in them. But Kevin Feldman had sold out and basically would do anything to keep himself in the spotlight. And this? That's exactly what it felt like. That this was just another project for him to get his name in the media and try to regain the fame he had lost when he hit puberty and started making really bad movies. I couldn't figure out for the life of me *why* my dad thought we would care about anything Kevin Feldman had to say.

It seemed like we had seen a hundred flyers by the time we made it down to the lake. There were already a bunch of kids there. I had to practically step over a couple sprawled out by the fire pit. They were so into each other . . . and wrapped around each other that they didn't notice me anyway.

"Hey, Ben," I called out as I passed. He waved a hand in my direction without disentangling himself from the girl. I couldn't tell who she was from this angle. But I figured I'd hear about it later. Secrets are pretty hard to keep on the rez.

Charlie and Jasper settled down beside a group of kids and started talking about Kevin Feldman. I nodded at a girl named Ingrid and sat down alone. I pulled the flyer out of my pocket and smoothed it on my leg. What was my dad *doing*? I stared at it for a second, then shook my head and crumpled it up again, throwing the paper into the fire.

Normally I liked hanging out with my friends by the lake. But today . . . I just couldn't do it. I thought maybe I should go see what Mouse was doing. I had promised him I'd take him fishing and I didn't want him to think I was just blowing smoke.

"I'm off to Mouse's," I called out to Charlie and Jasper. Jas was deep in conversation but Charlie looked up and cocked an eyebrow at me. I shrugged at him and he nodded back. Sometimes it's good to have friends you don't even have to explain yourself to. Or say anything at all.

This is the transcript of an actual scene from one of Kevin Feldman's horrible B-movies:

Fade in on a couple, standing in the doorway of a house. Soft light shines from the room behind them and the sound of rain can be heard.

Kevin Feldman: I wish we had more time together.

Random blonde chick in bikini: You could spend the night.

KF: I wish I could, baby. I know you need me. But the United States Postal Service needs me more.

RBCIB: Stay. Please stay. You're in danger out there.

KF: I know, baby. I know.

RBCIB: Then you'll stay?

KF: I can't. If I don't risk my life out there, people don't get their mail.

What the hell was my father thinking? True, I didn't have any first-hand knowledge of their grand plan. But there was no way this wasn't just another lame attempt by Kevin Feldman to be relevant. It was kind of his thing. He had been on a Save the Wild Horses kick for about a minute and the press actually showed up. But not for him. He had jumped on the bandwagon when Katy Perry had already started raising awareness. Then it was global warming. But Leonardo DiCaprio already had the market cornered on that one. So no one bothered with Feldman or the godawful anthem he had written.

I wasn't the only one who thought Kevin Feldman was a joke. There was a meme floating around for a while that said "Save the Wild Horses" with a picture of Feldman's face pasted on a horse's ass. It was pretty funny actually.

And my father had brought him here to "help"?

Chapter 14
HOME FROM AWAY

Following the road away from the lake, I started back toward Mouse's place. I took the shortcut through Mr. and Mrs. Maynard's field. The dozen or so cows that the Maynards owned, looked up as I passed. One, a jersey named Dolly I knew well from prior shortcuts, followed me across the field and kept pace with me step for step. I reached out and touched her side. I patted her warm flank and listened to her chew her cud as she walked.

"You're a good old cow, Dolly," I said. Yes, I talked to the cow. She seemed to like it. She tilted her head and brushed her wet nose against me. We were coming to the gate at the end of the road . . . the end of the line for Dolly. I gave her one last pat and vaulted the fence smoothly.

Mouse lived about a five-minute walk down the road from the Maynards. I'd only gone half that distance when I could see the rusted out tractor in the front yard that had come with the place. Seriously. The previous owners, a family called Running Deer, had abandoned it when it stopped running one day. There it sat for the next eight years, until Mouse's family moved across the rez. For some reason, they decided to leave the tractor where it sat. It had become a bit of a joke. Mouse's father, John, often said he was going to fix it up someday and drive it to church. But as the years passed and the tractor looked more and more like the rusted skeleton of a movie monster from one of Jasper's DVDs, it seemed less and less likely to ever happen.

And there it was, a dry heap of metal, surrounded by grass grown waist high and starting to sink into the ground. I laughed. I couldn't help it. I was picturing that heap being driven across the rez, belching smoke and scaring little kids.

I took the front steps two at a time and knocked. I could hear music coming from inside. Pop music. I knocked harder.

"Mouse! What the hell are you listening to, man? Turn that crap off and let me in!"

The door opened and I looked down, reaching out to mess up Mouse's hair in my usual greeting. But instead of Mouse's eager, open face, an exotic — and female — one looked right back at me.

My hand hung there between me and the face that wasn't Mouse's. I couldn't seem to make my mouth close. I saw almond-shaped eyes, tipped up at the edges and full of laughter. I saw full ruby red lips. I couldn't help but imagine myself kissing them. *Wait a second! Where did that come from? Floyd, Jeez! Close your mouth!*

I snatched my hand back and shoved it into my pocket. The person who wasn't Mouse leaned against the door. She looked at me with a playful smile tugging at the corners of her mouth.

Damn it! Say something, Floyd!

She smiled at my obvious discomfort and tossed her glossy black hair.

"Mouse! Floyd's here!" she called back over her shoulder.

My mouth dropped open again as she turned away, leaving me staring at an empty doorway.

"Wha?" *Oh, good. Smooth, Floyd. The most beautiful girl in the world has clearly heard stories of your cunning and intellect.*

And all you can manage is "wha?" This was so not how I pictured meeting the girl of my dreams. Instead of an orchestra playing, Selena Gomez was hitting a high note in the background.

"Hey, Floyd! Are you ready? Are we meeting Charlie and Jasper? Or is it just us today? 'Cause that's ok too. What are we doing? You said we'd go fishing. Are we fishing? I bet the fish are really biting today, dontcha think?" Mouse was bouncing around in front of me like a cartoon puppy. He was talking so fast it took every bit of concentration I had to make out what he was saying. All I could do was smile and nod. It didn't help that I was still feeling a bit dazed.

"We'll be back later with lots of fish, Kaya," Mouse said to the vision who glided back into view behind him.

"*Kaya?*" I spluttered in shock. As her chocolate brown eyes settled back on me, an amused smile lit up her face. *Oh God. Did I just say that out loud?*

She leaned over and gave Mouse a quick kiss on the cheek. I felt my face burning as she glanced at me again.

"Have fun," she said. Then she was gone.

I stared at Mouse. "*Kaya?*" I blurted out again. "That's your *sister?*"

"Yeah. She's back from school for the summer. Didn't you recognize her?"

"Mouse! The last time I saw her she was a foot shorter. She had braces and glasses and . . . that's your sister?" *Oh God. Shut up, Floyd!*

Mouse looked at me blankly, holding a fishing rod in one hand and a wicker creel in the other.

I cleared my throat . . . if only to break the awkward silence. "So yeah, man . . . I hear the fish are really biting today." I watched Mouse's face light up excitedly.

"My mom already mixed up a batch of her fish fry, just in case. I told her you were going to take me fishing soon. Are you gonna stay for supper, Floyd?"

"Uh . . ." What the hell is wrong with me? She's just a girl! I couldn't stop my hands from shaking or my stomach from jumping around at the thought of spending a couple of hours sitting around Mouse's place with Kaya. I saw myself making her laugh so I could see that smile again. Then I noticed Mouse staring. So I pulled myself out of the daydream of my James Bond-like coolness. In the daydream, I hadn't gawked at Kaya and said "wha?" to her. I had been suave and sexy. I had made her laugh. I had smiled at her with utter coolness and won her over with my killer charm.

Nope. I had said "wha?" I shook my head and smiled at Mouse, hoping desperately I'd get a second chance to show Kaya I wasn't a total dork.

"Yeah, sure, Mouse. But maybe we should catch the fish first, okay?"

Chapter 15
RODNEY

Mouse talked non-stop on the walk down to the lake. He talked while we were untying his Dad's boat from the dock. He talked while I pulled the starter cord on the boat motor. And he talked while I steered us onto the lake and toward my favourite fishing spot.

We settled into a routine easily, leaning back and casting out over the sparkling lake. The fish were biting and we were reeling them in steadily.

"So, Floyd," Mouse didn't even turn away from his pole and line as he spoke. I had to admire his dedication. "What do you think the biggest fish they ever caught here was?"

"Funny you should ask, Mouse. Haven't you ever heard the old timers talk about Rodney?"

"Rodney?" That got Mouse to look up for a second. "Who's Rodney?"

"You really don't know who Rodney is?" I was dragging out the suspense, enjoying stringing Mouse along.

"No." Mouse stared at me with his mouth open.

Man, this was going to be fun. "Dude," I said, "I can't believe you've never heard of Rodney! Rodney is the biggest trout in the lake, man! He's the Granddaddy fish. The Great Granddaddy even. He's the O.G.F., man! The Original Gangster Fish. I first heard about Rodney from my Nimosôm, my mom's Dad, back in the day."

"Really, Floyd? Tell me!" Mouse was practically bouncing beside me. He probably would have been bouncing for real if it wouldn't have tipped the boat.

"Nimosôm told me that he and *his* dad went fishing right here when he was a kid, in this exact same spot. So they're sitting around and shooting the breeze, right? They were eating sandwiches, and Nimosôm had his favourite. Ham and cheese on rye. So check this out . . . Nimosôm decides to add some of the sandwich to the hook. . . for bait."

"Right . . . go on, Floyd!" Mouse was hanging on my every word. Time to reel him in.

"So they're fishing and my Nimosôm feels this tug on his line. He looks down and feels it again. He leans over and sees something way down there, right? And all of a sudden, the line is almost pulled out of his hand!"

"Holy cow!" Mouse was on his feet, his pole forgotten.

"So he's fighting with this fish, right? And his dad is cheering him on and slapping him on the shoulder and yelling at him to pull that fish in. So Nimosôm is pulling and fighting and trying to reel this sucker in. And it's fighting him, man . . . it's going crazy!"

"Yeah? Then what, Floyd? What happened? Did your grandfather get Rodney?" Mouse was in danger of falling out of the boat. I had to lean over and grab his arm to make him sit back down before he sent us both into the water. I waited until he got himself settled and then went on.

"So Nimosôm is fighting with Rodney, trying to reel him in. His dad is leaning over the side of the boat with a net, waiting until the fish is close enough to the surface to grab him. Nimosôm's hands and arms are tired. But he's still fighting. There's no way he's going to give up this fish. His pole is bent almost double, that trout is so incredibly heavy, right? His shoulders are burning . . . his neck muscles are all bunched up. He's being pulled forward over the edge of the boat, but he's not giving up!"

"Right . . . so what did he do, Floyd? Did he get the fish?"

I smiled, enjoying this as much as Mouse was. "So he's been fighting this fish for an hour. He's exhausted and he doesn't know if he can keep it up . . . even with his dad there, telling him what an awesome job he's doing. So right when he doesn't think he can fight anymore, he gives this almighty pull. It brings Rodney close enough to the surface for his Dad to reach down and get the net under him."

"YEAH!" Mouse punched one fist into the air, threatening to throw us overboard again. "They got him! Poor old Rodney!"

I reached out to steady him before continuing. "Well that's just it . . . they *had* him. So my Great-grandfather gets Rodney in the net and they're screaming and hollering and they pull him in. And that sucker is HUGE! They'd never seen a lake trout that size. They'd never even *heard* of one that big. Nimosôm said Rodney was a hundred pounds for sure."

"A hundred pounds? Holy cow, Floyd! What happened?" I was thankful that Mouse stayed sitting down this time.

"So they had him in the bottom of the boat. And Rodney was thrashing around all over the place. Do you have any idea how big a hundred-pound fish is, man? It was taking up so much of the boat that there was almost no room left for them! So they're panicking because Rodney is flopping around like . . . like . . . well, like a fish out of water. They're backing up as far as they can. And Rodney is jumping and flailing. And the boat is rocking. And with one last giant leap across the boat, Rodney hits the side and they capsize!"

"Oh my GOD!" Mouse was on his feet again. I grabbed at him and pushed him back down before he capsized *us*.

"So there they were, bobbing in the lake like a couple of loons, watching Rodney swimming away. The biggest, freakin' lake trout ever caught and they lost him."

"Wow," breathed Mouse. "They must have freaked out."

"Yeah. They did. But what could they do? At least both of them had seen him, so they could vouch for each other. You know? People *had* to believe them. They both spent the rest of their lives looking for Rodney, man. So did everyone else around here. Lots of people have seen him. A few have even had him on the hook. But no one has ever reeled him in since then."

I sat back and watched Mouse's face. His mouth was hanging open and his pole still sat forgotten by his feet.

"Wow," Mouse breathed. "We have to catch him, Floyd! Have you ever seen him? Man, can you imagine if we got him? My dad would die, man! And Charlie and Jasper would completely lose their minds! Should we tell them? Do you think they'd want to try to get him too?" Mouse's voice was getting louder and more excited with every word.

I laughed. "Slow down! Your dad would definitely die, Mouse. But let's not tell Jasper and Charlie, okay? Let's keep this between you and me. Our secret."

If it was possible, Mouse's smile got even bigger. "Okay, Floyd. I won't tell a soul. But we totally have to come back here and find Rodney."

"For sure, Mouse. And we have the secret weapon."

"What's that?"

"Ham and cheese on rye, man! Rodney's favourite."

Mouse was still talking away about his plans to catch Rodney. But my mind was racing. I knew that storytelling was something I was good at. I had been entertaining people with stories for years — I liked the idea that I was a storyteller. Storytellers are traditionally the ones who keep our history alive. I had wanted to be a writer for as long as I could remember. And it was important to me to keep our culture alive. But maybe it didn't have to only be through *traditional* storytelling. Maybe I didn't have to just tell trickster stories or other legends to be a storyteller. Maybe I could just be a voice for us. Maybe our stories of the rez and how people felt — and even how sometimes people gave up — defined who we were just as much. Maybe the stories we were living were just as important as the ones we had already lived.

Chapter 16
MOUSE'S HOUSE

The river gods were generous. The fish were all but jumping into the boat all afternoon. Mouse did a little dance and set the boat rocking every time he reeled one in. He never got tired of celebrating his catch. He exclaimed every time that *this* had to be the biggest lake trout ever caught. Except for Rodney, of course.

"Floyd! Check this one out, man! Have you ever seen such a beauty?" he would shout, as he held up his latest catch for my approval. I *had* seen such a beauty before. Ten minutes earlier, when he showed me the last one. But I dutifully smiled and told him how amazing each and every fish was.

It seemed like no time had passed before Mouse's creel was full of fat trout. I was shocked to find that we had been fishing for almost five hours. Wow. Time really did fly when you were having fun.

"Floyd?" Mouse's voice snapped me back into reality. I turned to see him hitching his very full creel over his shoulder. "Are you ready?"

"Yeah, Mouse. I think we've got enough to feed the whole rez here."

Mouse laughed. I could see he was picturing everyone sitting around his mom's kitchen, eating fish dipped in her famous fish fry. It was a recipe that she refused to share.

I knew that every woman and quite a few men had tried to get it out of her at one time or another.

"So I can tell my dad about Rodney, right? I mean, he probably already knows about him, anyway. Do you think? He's never mentioned Rodney to me, but that doesn't mean anything. And if he does know about Rodney, then maybe he and I can fish for him sometime. You know . . . when you can't go out with me. That's okay, right? You don't mind, do you? Anyway, I bet he's already heard of Rodney. Maybe he's even hooked him, Floyd. Do you think so? 'Cause Dad's a great fisherman. I bet he has."

Mouse kept up a steady stream of chatter as we walked back to his place. I found that I really didn't have to contribute too much to the conversation. Just the odd "oh yeah?" and "mm hmm" kept him pretty happy.

As I watched Mouse gesturing and laughing, I couldn't help but think of his sister again. I had never taken much notice of her when she lived here. Why would I? She always had her nose stuck in a book. Her hair pulled into a messy ponytail with little pieces sticking up in crazy horns all over her head and her thick glasses made her look like an owl. A surprised owl if you talked to her and caught her off guard. She was nice enough, I guess. But back then when she smiled, there was so much metal in her mouth that if the sun happened to be shining and caught her braces the right way, you were almost blinded. I had never even really noticed she was a *girl* before. But now the braces and glasses were gone. And her hair hung like a shining curtain of ebony down her back.

Oh my God. Did I really just think that? What is wrong with me? "A shining curtain of ebony"? Where the hell did that come from? I see a pretty girl and suddenly I'm Shakespeare?

I felt a sharp elbow in my ribs and looked down. Mouse.

Right. *He has the same eyes as his sister. Oh, for crying out loud! Stop it, Floyd!*

Mouse asked, "Should we clean them all now or freeze some, Floyd?"

"May as well clean them. There's four of you, plus me. I don't know about you, but I'm hungry! I could eat most of these trout myself, heads and all!"

Mouse led me around the back of the house where a board was set up across a plastic garbage can. His dad was by the shed, splitting logs into kindling with an axe. He was singing something as he worked and shaking his butt a little. It sounded suspiciously like the song that had been playing when I picked Mouse up that morning. Ah, man. I couldn't help but relax when I visited Mouse's place. Unlike Mouse, John was a veritable giant. But he was as easygoing as his son. He was quick to smile and always ready to lend a hand.

"You boys need a hand with the cleaning?" he called out, proving my point. He wiped the sweat from his forehead.

"Nah, we're good, Dad," answered Mouse.

"Were they biting today?"

"Yeah! We got some of the biggest lake trout I've ever seen! One of them is for sure fifteen pounds, right, Floyd?"

I couldn't believe how easily they spoke to each other. I found myself wishing my dad was more like John.

"Maybe even twenty," I said. I held out my hands to show how big that particular fish was.

John smiled and walked over to clap a hand on Mouse's shoulder. Then he turned to me. "Staying for supper, Floyd?"

I nodded, smiling back. "I've just gotta call my mom first."

"I heard your Dad is under the weather. Why don't you tell your mom to join us for dinner as well?"

Under the weather. Right. Apparently that was code for stressed out and planning meetings with movie stars. "I will. Thanks, John."

Mouse grabbed the biggest fish from the creel and slapped it down on the board, picking up a sharp knife in his other hand. In one quick motion, he slit the belly of the fish open and pulled the guts out of it. Then he passed it over to me to fillet. We were a good team and had all of the fish cleaned and filleted in no time. My stomach was growling and I could almost taste dinner already as John took the catch in to Raynetta to prepare.

"We better get cleaned up, Mouse." I led the way into the house and went into the bathroom. Mouse continued on to his bedroom at the far end of the hall. That was likely where Kaya's bedroom was as well. But I couldn't let myself go where that thought was leading.

I soaped up my hands and arms well, washing away the clean smell of fresh fish and the scales that had flecked off and clung to my skin. I rinsed the lather away and leaned over the sink, looking at my reflection in the mirror and smoothing my hair. Then I texted my mom to let her know where I was and to pass on John's invitation for dinner.

There was a knock on the bathroom door.

"Floyd? Are you done in there yet?" Mouse called out.

"Yeah, Mouse. I'm done." I opened the door, shaking off my thoughts of family — mine and Mouse's. I walked to the kitchen, following the mouth-watering smells of fish sizzling in oil and butter melting over garden fresh beans.

"Mouse! Hurry up!" I called over my shoulder. My phone dinged and I read the text without pausing. "Hey, John, Mom is at Auntie Martha's for dinner. But she asked me to thank you for asking."

"No problem. Floyd, have you ever smelled anything as amazing as my wife's fish fry?" He put his arms around Raynetta from behind.

She leaned her head back and gave him a quick kiss on the cheek. "Get out of this kitchen, you two. Let me finish up the fish so I can get it to the table. Shoo!" She turned and flicked at John with the dish towel. He pulled her ponytail and then grabbed my arm. He yanked me out of the room with him and plopped himself down at the head of the table.

"Come on, woman!" he shouted. "Bring me my dinner!"

Chapter 17
WHISPERS

Dinner at Mouse's house was full of laughter. They seemed happy. They were polite to each other and listened to what each had to say about their day.

Mouse was, of course, full of stories about our adventures fishing. John talked about his ideas for landscaping around the tractor out front. Raynetta smiled at him and I couldn't look away as he took her hand and raised it to his lips.

I ate quietly, glancing up now and then at Kaya. She was laughing good-naturedly at her brother and smiled back at me when she caught me looking.

"The fish is wonderful, Floyd. You boys did a great job. Now everyone, pe mitso! Eat!" Raynetta said.

I smiled back at her, pleased to be singled out as a provider. They were all so easy to be around. I couldn't get used to how nice they were to each other. I mean, my parents were nice. We didn't have any of the family issues that a lot of people on the rez had. But lately we hadn't had much to say to each other. We'd all been in our own little worlds.

"So any idea what your dad is doing . . . you know . . . with everything that's going on?" John asked through a forkful of salad.

"John!" Raynetta tried to shush him.

"What? We need to be able to talk about this stuff. That's the only way it's going to get better."

"Dad is right," Kaya said.

He was, actually. Half the problem was that no one seemed to be talking about what we could do. Especially my dad. I had a feeling that his silence had something to do with his past at school. He had to have learned young that if something was wrong, you kept it to yourself or suffered the consequences.

"If more people were talking about this, maybe someone would do something. Someone needs to get us some help," Kaya continued.

I saw Raynetta look at me uncomfortably.

I knew I had to say something. "Well . . . I mean, my dad is trying to do something . . ." I trailed off. To be honest, I didn't have a clue what he was doing. He kept saying he and the Council had plans to help everyone. But so far, I wasn't seeing any follow through.

"I'm sure he is, sweetheart," Raynetta said to me. She frowned at her husband and changed the subject. "So how's your mother, Floyd?"

Dinner passed quickly for me after that. I laughed at Mouse's jokes. My face hurt from smiling so much. After eating like there was no tomorrow, and polishing off seconds of dessert and coffee, I pushed back from the table and patted my full stomach. John and Mouse did the same.

"That was a great supper, sweetheart," John said, smiling at his wife. I watched as she gazed back warmly and began clearing the dishes from the table. She went to the kitchen and Kaya followed her.

Mouse and his father were talking about a soccer game they

had watched together the week before. John was promising to practice in the backyard with his son that weekend. I watched as he leaned over and engulfed his son in a warm, one-armed hug. John hadn't been to residential school or have the pressure of leading a community on his shoulders. Maybe that's what had made my father more reserved. Less affectionate. Less likely to smile and hug his son.

"Mouse," said John, "you better go hose down the cleaning station outside. Floyd and I can finish clearing up in here."

"Okay, Dad. I'll be back in a minute." He raced off. Mouse only seemed to have one speed. FAST.

I stood up and grabbed the platter of fish bones . . . all that was left after the hungry vultures had descended on it. I took it and what was left of the bowl of green beans with me as I followed John toward the kitchen. I guess I wasn't paying close enough attention. When John stopped suddenly, I walked right into his back, spilling a shower of leftover fish bits on his shirt.

"Oh, sor—"

"SHHHHH!" He slapped a meaty hand over my open mouth and gestured frantically toward the kitchen with a bowl of mashed potatoes. I nodded, trying to show that I understood and hoping against hope that he would take his hand off my mouth. It was so big he was also covering my nose and I couldn't breathe. As he let go, I drew a deep, grateful breath. I wondered for the millionth time how a giant like John could possibly have fathered a little guy like Mouse.

John held a finger up to his lips. He was dancing from foot to foot and waving madly toward the kitchen. Okay then. Now I saw the resemblance to his son.

John leaned toward the swinging door and nearly yanked me off my feet, pulling me forward with him. Raynetta and

Kaya were doing the dishes. I could hear the water running into the sink and dishes clattering together. I could also hear them talking. Loudly. Raynetta was clearly in the middle of some kind of monologue.

"Kaya, isn't Floyd funny and smart? And he is so sweet with Mouse." *Wait. What?* They were talking about me. I looked up at John and he grinned back.

"I know, Mom," I heard Kaya answer. "He's nice, okay? Can we please stop talking about him now?"

"Did you see him when he came in with Mouse? He's so handsome. And he'd make such a great boyfriend."

Oh. My. God. Mouse's mom was pimping me out.

"MOM! For god's sake! What are you? Thirteen?"

John was doubled over, silently laughing. He reached over and smacked me on the ass. Nice.

"What? I'm just saying that Floyd is a good boy. And good looking too," Raynetta shot back.

"I can't believe I'm having this conversation with my mother. Okay! Miwapewiw! Are you happy now?"

My face was on fire. Kaya thought I was handsome. KAYA THOUGHT I WAS HANDSOME! John shot me a silent high five and nodded back toward the dining room. Time to back out before we got caught eavesdropping.

"Hey, guys!" Mouse was speaking way too loudly as he wandered in from the other room. "What are you doing just standing out here?"

There was silence from the kitchen. I hoped the ground would choose that moment to open up and swallow me whole. Mouse pushed open the door and held it for me and his dad to enter the kitchen. It gave his mom and sister a clear view of John's grinning face and my scarlet one. I could see that Kaya's face had gone completely white. What a pair we made. She was looking down, so I couldn't see her eyes. I can't say I blamed her.

"We didn't hear anything," John blurted out.

Raynetta rolled her eyes at him, and cleared her throat. "Well, come on. Bring those dishes in. They're not going to clear themselves."

Dear Diary

Dear Journal

Dear WhoeverIdontcarewho

She likes me.

She actually likes me.

Me!

Suddenly, I can feel that dark cloud that's been following me around lifting. Instead of being rooted in the past, I finally feel some kind of hope for my future.

And I want Kaya to be part of it.

I keep thinking about different programs we could run for kids to help them connect to our culture. I wonder if kids other than Mouse would want to go fishing? Maybe we could have some kind of fishing derby? The one with the biggest fish would win a prize. And we could cook up all the fish we catch and have a potlatch. I know there are some people here who aren't doing so well. Old Mr. Simard can't hunt or fish anymore and his pension barely covers the bills. We could go back to the tribe mentality where everyone is taken care of and no one goes without what they need.

Going back to our roots could be a good thing for us — for my friends and for me. It could be a good thing for me and Kaya.

Chapter 18
AROUND THE FIRE

I left Mouse and his family and headed back to the lake. I knew the guys were still there from the texts I had been getting all evening. Sounded like there was a huge party raging on without me.

All I could think about on my walk to the lake was Kaya. I hadn't been interested in anyone for a while . . . since before Aaron had died. Losing one of my best friends and being the one who found his body kind of put me off romance for a while. Aaron had despaired of finding anyone to love on the rez. How could I not see how bad it was for him? How could I not save him? The guilt I felt had left me barely functional. And my father *still* hadn't realized how badly we needed some kind of counselling here.

I pushed the thought of Aaron away and focused on happier thoughts. Like the future. Like Kaya. I don't know what it was about her but she was in my head.

Another neon flyer fluttered past, caught in an updraft. I grabbed at it. Another stupid flyer for my dad's project with Kevin Feldman. I rolled my eyes, shaking my head. I just didn't get it.

Everyone down by the lake was apparently wondering the

same thing. As I walked up to the bonfire, I heard a bunch of kids talking about it.

"What do you think Kevin Feldman is going to say?" someone asked.

I spotted Charlie through the flames. "I don't know, man. But Floyd's dad must know what he's doing."

I was impressed that Charlie was standing up for my dad. Charlie knew as well as I did that Dad didn't have a clue what he was doing.

"But Feldman's a loser!" another kid said.

"Yeah, he is. But maybe he's got some good ideas or something."

"Kevin Feldman hasn't done anything good since he made that horror movie when he was fourteen. It's been downhill for him since then."

"Yeah!" a chorus of voices rang out.

I was about to call out to Charlie when someone's voice broke into the jeers.

"I hear he's coming here to make a movie."

I stopped in my tracks.

"What? What movie?" Charlie asked.

"I heard my dad talking to my mom." It was Ben, the guy I had seen with a girl wrapped around him earlier. His father was on the Council with my dad.

"And?"

"So the talk is that Feldman is obsessed with *The Revenant*. Totally thinks he should have played the DiCaprio part." There was a round of laughter at that. "He wants to make another blockbuster just like it. But this time he'd be the star."

"So, he wants to remake an Oscar-winning movie into some lame B-movie with D-list actors and a tiny budget?" Charlie asked. "Why is he coming here to do that?"

"He wants to make it here because none of the other reserves would let him. I heard that he saw the news reports of that other reserve up north . . . the one under the water advisory? He called them first. When they said no, he called the one that's been on the news for a suicide epidemic. They said no too. No one else would let him film on their land. So he called us and we said yes. I think he wants us to be the extras."

Wait a second. My dad was going to let this guy come in and use us to make his crappy movie?

The group had erupted into loud insulting comments about Feldman. The kind of comments that would result in one of his famous slander lawsuits.

"I'm so getting discovered!" Jasper was crowing, posing and strutting around like he was holding an Oscar. "I'd like to thank all of the little people . . ."

"My dad doesn't think we should let him do it," Ben said over the din.

"Why?" Jasper demanded. "This could be my big break!"

The statement was met by hoots from the other kids.

"Because my dad said it's a joke, only Feldman doesn't get it. It's like an old cowboys and Indians movie. It makes fun of us. A bunch of drunk Indians saved by the white man. It basically cashes in on every single cliché there is."

"Yeah, well, *my* dad says they'd have to cut down all the trees along the lake to make room for the trailers and equipment and stuff," a girl added.

"Not just for the equipment," Ben said.

"What do you mean?" Charlie asked him.

"It's supposed to take place on the plains. So they want to raze the forest around the lake in every direction."

Oh god. What was my father *thinking*? Yeah, maybe it would bring money in. But at what cost? The money would dry up soon enough and it wasn't going to help anyone in the long run. If anything, we'd come off looking stupid and lose an entire forest in the process. And it would probably keep us from getting funding and programs we desperately needed. My dad would let a Hollywood has-been destroy our home for that?

The conversation was in full swing. But instead of moving into the firelight and joining in, I stepped backward and walked away. There was no way I could defend my father this time. I didn't even want to try.

Part of a paper I wrote for school:

Crazy Horse yelled out "Hoka Hey! Today is a good day to die" before the Battle of Little Big Horn. If a warrior could die bravely and with honour, then he died a good death. So Crazy Horse felt that dying in battle, fighting for what he believed in, was honourable. That's what made it a good day to die. The phrase would be used for centuries by tribes everywhere.

Chapter 19
KAYA

I went to bed that night thinking about Kaya. I woke up the next morning, still thinking about her. The way she smiled at me. The way she laughed. The way her hair hung over her shoulders. It was mortifying. I was turning into some kind of Romeo or something. I was seventeen, so it wasn't like I hadn't had girlfriends before. But Kaya was different. She was smart and funny. She was so beautiful that I couldn't think of anything but her eyes and her lips and the way they turned up slowly into a soft smile that lit up her entire face. See? Freakin' Romeo. Next thing, I'd be composing sonnets and writing love songs. But thinking about Kaya kept me from thinking about my dad and what he was doing with Kevin Feldman. And what he *wasn't* doing for our people.

I was standing at the kitchen counter making a turkey sandwich and singing along to the radio. My mom liked Q107 — Toronto's Best Rock according to the DJ. My mom was dusting in the living room and the Rolling Stones and I were singing about getting no satisfaction, when the doorbell rang.

"I'll get it," my mom said. She headed over to the door while I spread mayo on the bread and slapped turkey and lettuce down on top. I was cutting a tomato and doing a little dance along to the music. Then I heard a throat being cleared behind me. I did a little spin à la Mick Jagger and came face to face with Kaya. *Oh, come on! Do I ALWAYS have to look like a complete dork in front of her?*

Kaya's mouth was twitching. I couldn't look away. A slow smile crept across her face. To her credit, she looked like she was trying not to laugh. My face, meanwhile, was about to burst into flame.

"Hi," she said without breaking eye contact.

"Hi." *Oh good. A brilliant response.* Where the hell was Romeo when I needed him?

"I was walking by and I thought I'd stop in. Say hi."

"Oh. Hi." Yup, said that already. "Well . . . maybe I can walk you home?" *Better, Floyd.*

"Yeah. I'd like that."

"Cool."

I wrapped my sandwich in foil and put it in the fridge for later. In the grand scheme of things, this was definitely more important than food. I smiled at Kaya, taking a deep breath and willing my hands to stop shaking.

"Ready?"

× × ×

I wasn't always the smoothest talker but I found that I didn't have to try too hard with Kaya. She made it easy for me to talk about things like my boring high school and my friends. And any time I found myself at a loss for words, she had something to talk about. Her fancy performing arts school. Mouse. Books. Music. Movies. It turned out we liked a lot of the same things. Once I got past the fact that she was the most beautiful girl I had ever seen, she was actually pretty cool.

"So Charlie has a thing for superheroes?" she laughed.

"Not just a thing. It's more like an obsession. Like who could beat who in a fight . . . that kind of thing."

She laughed out loud. Man, she had a great laugh. I could listen to her laughing all day.

"Like who? Who does Charlie see in the big match-up?"

"Well he had this thing recently about whether Wonder Woman could kick a guy's ass."

"What? Of course she could! Just because she's a woman . . . she's still WONDER Woman, for crying out loud!"

"Clearly I better keep the two of you away from each other. You guys might come to blows."

"Well who did he want her to fight? At least tell me that?"

"Oh man, I don't remember. I think he had her going up against Iron Man or something."

"Well that's just stupid. He's not even a real superhero. He just has a lot of money and a cool suit."

I was pretty sure I had a dopey smile on my face by then. I tried to rearrange my features into something slightly cooler.

I failed.

She kicked at a stone with the toe of her shoe, then kicked a bigger one to me. I dribbled it from foot to foot and sent it back. She stopped it, then drew her leg back and sent it flying into a tree with a powerful kick.

"Whoa! A soccer player like your brother?" I applauded loudly.

"Who do you think taught him how to play?" She leaned her shoulder against me for a second. Before I could react to the unexpected contact, I felt her tiny, soft hand slip into mine. I glanced at her in surprise. Okay, more like in total and utter shock. I couldn't have been more surprised if . . . I don't know. If I found out the zombie apocalypse was real. Or if I won a thousand dollars a week for life on one of those lottery scratchers or something.

She was looking down at her feet as we walked. Her cheeks were pink and she was clearly avoiding eye contact. I squeezed her hand gently and smiled. Our eyes met. I don't think it would be a lie to say that I definitely heard music . . . and saw a few fireworks. And that was just from holding her hand. I suddenly realized that we had been quiet for a few minutes . . . and I didn't want her to feel awkward.

"So . . . uh . . . you've been back for the whole summer?" Why hadn't I seen her before now?

"No. I spent some time with my Aunt and Uncle in Toronto. I got into a summer arts program there."

"Art? That's cool. Do you paint?" This girl just kept getting better and better. She laughed that tinkling laugh that made me feel like I was the greatest man alive.

"No, it's an acting program for First Nations youth."

"Right! Of course. You're in theatre school. That sounds cool."

She smiled up at me. It was amazing that she didn't seem to think I was an idiot.

"Performing arts school," she corrected. "And it was. I was doing a lot of plays at my school and a few productions outside of it too. But this summer program was so much better. Everyone was so talented! They made us work harder than I thought was possible. But it was so worth it. I loved it." She was glowing. I could see her passion in her face. I felt like I could almost reach out and touch it.

"That's amazing," I said. The funny thing was that I meant it with all my heart.

"Yeah. We had the most incredible guest teachers. Adam Beach and Jennifer Podemski worked with us. We worked on some movement exercises with Michael Greyeyes. And they even had Tomson Highway come in!"

I perked up. I actually knew those names! Especially the last one. "You're kidding! Tomson Highway is my favourite writer!"

She looked surprised, but I forged on. "I mean, I loved *The Rez Sisters*. But *Dry Lips Oughta Move to Kapuskasing* is the funniest play I've ever read! I actually thought about trying to get some of my friends together for a reading or something. Tomson Highway is the reason I want to be a writer!"

Oops. Ah hell. Did I just say that out loud? I flushed, looking away.

Kaya stopped in her tracks and faced me. "You're a writer?"

"No. I mean, I'd like to be. I read a lot. I do some writing at night sometimes. Short stories. And I have a journal. I'm not sure I'm any good at it. I just . . ." I trailed off, not looking at her. "I've never really talked about it . . . the writing," I finished lamely.

"Maybe you'll write a play for me someday." She smiled.

"Maybe I will," I told her. *Hey, you never know.* "I'd write something important, just like Tomson. He knows, man. He knows how important it is to tell our stories, you know?"

"That's why the summer arts program was so important to me. I was learning from Indigenous artists who want to pass on our culture and tell our stories!"

"Yes! Tomson Highway writes about people just like us. All of this?" I spun my arms around in a circle, taking in the rez around me, all the people living on it. "All of this, everyone we see every single day and all the boring old stuff we do? It's real. All of our stories should be told! And it's people like us who need to tell them."

"Maybe we could work on something together," Kaya ventured.

"Definitely!"

"I think we should write about Aaron . . . and those five girls . . . and everyone we've lost. We could tell their stories. Not just with words, but with music and movement and art. Telling the rest of the world the things that are a part of who we are . . . that's how we honour all of them."

I was nodding. "Yes. We honour them by sharing who they were to us. But also by giving them a voice they didn't feel like they had."

"Right. And not just who they were. Who *we* are. The people they left behind. How they left us. How we're still here. *Hoka Hey!*"

I looked at her, surprised. "Today is a good day to die," I said.

She tilted her head and studied me. "Not today, Floyd. Today we live. For them and for us."

She stood on her tiptoes and kissed me on the cheek. As she turned to continue our walk, I reached out and grabbed her hand. I didn't think. I didn't consider the consequences. For once, I just acted. I pulled her back toward me. As she looked up curiously, I reached out and brushed the hair away from her face. I had wanted to touch her face since I saw her open the door at her house. Before I could think or change my mind, I leaned down and kissed her.

I half expected her to pull away, to punch me in the face even. But I felt her lips kissing me back and I never wanted that moment to end.

My life may not be easy and things are about as far as you can get from perfect. But right at that moment, there wasn't a thing I'd change about it.

My Future — by Floyd Twofeathers, Grade Seven

I want to be a writer. I want to write down stories that people remember. I want to pass on stories just like my ancestors passed their stories on. I'm going to be a writer like Tomson Highway and share important stories about our culture. Tomson Highway says that he writes in Cree in his head and his heart. I want to write with my head and my heart too. But in English. Storytelling is an important part of my culture. Storytellers pass on history and tradition. I read somewhere that stories help us cope with adversity. I want to write stories that make a difference somehow.

Chapter 20
LOSING THE FUTURE

Like I had the night before, I went to bed thinking about Kaya. I had stayed up late, trying to find something amazing for her to read. I had a pile of notebooks full of my writing to go through. But I wanted whatever I chose for her to read to be perfect. I'm pretty sure I went to sleep with a smile on my face. I know I woke up with one.

It didn't last long.

My parents were both sitting at the table when I walked into the kitchen. Breakfast together was becoming more and more rare.

"Good morning," I said, still smiling widely. Then I noticed the grim looks on both of their faces. I felt the smile slide off my own face. "What's wrong?" I asked.

"Mary Running Wolf died last night." My mother's voice broke.

"Oh no." It was all I could manage. Mary was a healer and people came from other reserves to get her medicines and advice. I had even heard she dabbled in things like love potions but that could have just been a rumour. My mom had apprenticed with Mary. She had spent years beside her, learning everything she knew about medicines and healing.

"I can't believe she's gone," my mother said, tears running down her face.

"What happened?" I asked. "Was it her heart?" Mary had suffered a heart attack a few months before. But I thought my mom had told me she was doing okay.

My mom shook her head, unable to speak.

"She killed herself," my father said. He put a protective arm around my mom.

"What? Why?" I didn't think until the words were out of my mouth. If anyone knew that you couldn't find an answer for someone's suicide, it was me. "I mean . . . I'm so sorry, Mom."

"She was sick," my mom said. "Sicker than we knew, I guess."

"She left a note for your mother," my dad added.

"I didn't know she was suffering like that," my mom said, crying. "I didn't know she felt like she couldn't help anyone anymore."

I didn't know what to say. I knew that the suicide epidemic was affecting everyone. But I never imagined that a woman like Mary — a healer — would do something like that. It scared me to think that no one was immune to this. We were losing teenagers, little kids, parents, brothers and sisters and elders. We were losing family. Our rez really was dying.

I had spent a lot of time thinking about how kids my age felt like they had no future and nothing to live for. But it hadn't occurred to me how their parents and grandparents might be feeling. Maybe they felt guilty for not being able to give their children more than they had. Maybe they felt like they had failed them.

No one could do anything about sickness and age. But if an elder like Mary felt useless, then maybe it was a problem we could do something about. If we could give kids hope for some kind of future, their parents and grandparents wouldn't feel like they were failing them. If elders could see their wisdom and learning being carried into the future by the kids, they would have something to hang on for. And maybe we wouldn't lose anyone else.

×   ×   ×

I left my parents at home. I wanted to stay with my mom but she insisted I go on with my day. She had to talk to some of Mary's friends and start making arrangements for her funeral.

I was supposed to hang out with the guys later. But I was free as a bird all morning. So I headed over to pick up Kaya for a walk.

I knocked on the door. I only had to wait about ten seconds before it was thrown wide open.

"Floyd!" Mouse stood in the doorway. He looked happy as anything to see me. "What are you doing here?"

"Uhhh . . ." I drew a complete blank. Of course I knew that Mouse lived there. But it hadn't occurred to me that he might open the door. Or that I'd have to explain that I wasn't there to see him.

"Are we hanging out?" he asked hopefully.

Ah jeez. Why hadn't I realized this might happen?

"Ummm. No. I mean . . ." Damn. This was not going well.

"Hi, Floyd." Kaya appeared behind Mouse. I felt my heart skip a beat. I glanced nervously at Mouse.

"I'm going for a walk with Kaya now, Mouse. But I told the guys I'd meet up with them later. I'll grab you before I head over, okay?"

Mouse's smiled dimmed for a second. He looked a little confused, like he couldn't figure out why I was going for a walk with his sister. But as soon as I mentioned coming back for him, he grinned.

"Okay. Have a good walk." He breezed away, leaving Kaya in the doorway and me on the porch. Staring at her.

"Ready?" she asked.

"Let's go."

She took my hand as soon as we got down the stairs. There was something so natural about it. She didn't play games or try to hide how she was feeling. She was different than any other girl I had dated.

But much as I was enjoying being with Kaya, I couldn't stop thinking about Mary and my mom. I knew that Mary's death — her suicide — had to have hit Mom really hard. I didn't know what I could do for her. But I had some pretty good ideas about what I could do to help other people like Mary. If I could get anyone to listen.

I walked through the rez, holding Kaya's hand and really looking at the people we passed. I noticed that there were more men than I had seen in a long time wearing their hair cut short, when there had always been a fair number of them who kept it long. When I pointed it out to Kaya, she nodded.

"Yeah, I noticed that as soon as I came home. They cut their braids off. They're all in mourning."

I was quiet for a minute, thinking about that. So many of us had lost someone. With the rez being such a small community, there was not a single person who hadn't been affected by suicide.

"Somebody needs to do something," Kaya was saying. "Something better than bringing Kevin Feldman in to shoot a movie."

She was right. But I still felt like I had to defend my dad. Even if I didn't fully believe in him myself right now.

"I think my dad is trying to come up with something to bring money in," I said, starting with what I knew was true. "And maybe . . . maybe that'll at least start to help? I think he wants to get some media attention. I'm sure he thinks that shooting a Hollywood movie here would do that?" It had turned into a question. Even I didn't think his grand plan with the big Hollywood has-been was going to do anything except embarrass all of us.

"How will that help, Floyd?" she asked softly. She wasn't trying to be unkind. But she didn't have any misplaced loyalty to my dad like I did.

"I don't know," I admitted.

Her voice stayed soft and kind, but she carried on. "How is that going to help save people like Mary? And those poor girls? And Aaron?" she asked. I squeezed her hand and walked on. I nodded at Mr. Henry watering his lawn and tried to ignore his missing braid.

When I was younger, five or six I think, kids used to bug me about my hair. "Why do you wear it long?" they'd ask. "Do you want to be a girl?" They'd laugh at me, pulling my hair when I walked past and calling me Floydina.

I hated it. I was just a kid and I still cared what people thought. I'd ride the bus home, tears in my eyes.

"I want to cut my hair," I told my father one night. I was sure that cutting off my hair to look like the other kids would make them accept me.

*My father looked up from whatever he was reading. He
studied me for almost a minute. A minute is a long time for
a little kid.*

*"Sit down, son," he finally said. He nodded toward a chair.
"If you want to cut your hair, you can."*

*"Good," I said. I was all ready to make a break for the
bathroom and grab the scissors.*

*"Do you know why we grow our hair and braid it?" he asked
before I could escape and start cutting.*

*I shrugged. I didn't care. I just wanted to fit in with the
other kids.*

*"Some people think it connects us with Creator. Some
think that a braid is a symbol of strength and wisdom.
Braided hair sets us apart and shows us as being a part of
our culture. I think it's all of those things. But for me, it's
also a symbol of pride. When I went away to school,
I was forced to cut my hair. So was your grandfather.
They cut our hair to strip us of our identity. When I left
school, I grew it out again. I wanted to make some kind
of statement. I was still the same person I had been. They
hadn't taken that away from me. They may have tried to
oppress us. But they couldn't take who I was away from
me. Do you understand?" he asked softly.*

I nodded slowly. "I think so," I told him.

"So if you want to cut your hair, it's your decision. But think about it first, okay?"

I promised him that I would. I meant it. I spent a long time that night lying in bed and thinking about what he had said.

I braided my hair the next morning and went to school with my head held high. I never thought about cutting my hair again.

Chapter 21
MAN TO MAN

I loved being with Kaya. I was quickly finding that I enjoyed it way more than I enjoyed anything else in my life. But I couldn't turn off my brain. Feldman was going to be here that night and I needed to talk to my dad about it. He was about to make a huge mistake that would affect everyone. Including him.

I walked to the Council office with more purpose than my usual meandering. I had to get to Dad before Feldman arrived. As I opened the door, I was met with what could only be described as a din. People were running around and yelling to each other. I had never seen the Council office like this. Half the people there weren't even on the Council. I saw Ben's father and nodded at him. He didn't look happy.

I followed the noise to my dad's office. He was yelling into his cellphone. I sat down and waited while he finished up his call.

"Floyd!" My dad slapped a hand on my back. Apparently his sadness at the loss of Mary had worn off. "To what do I owe this honour?" He was glowing. I had never seen him glow before. Then the smell of alcohol, masked by an overpowering scent of Listerine strips, hit me.

"Dad, I need to talk to you about this Kevin Feldman meeting," I said nervously. My dad never drank. I was so shocked, I almost changed my mind about talking to him. Almost.

"I really don't have time to talk, Floyd. We're going crazy around here trying to get ready for the meeting. What is it?"

"You can't do this, Dad. I know you're going to let him make a movie. But I also know what the movie is about. He's using us for publicity and you're letting him. It's going to make us look bad. It's going to make Indigenous people look stupid. And it's not going to bring attention to the real issues here. And while he's ruining us, he's going to destroy all the land around the lake." I blurted it all out. I hadn't even taken a breath.

My father looked at me, studied me. Then he stood up and held the door open. "Thanks for coming by, Floyd."

I didn't know what was happening. I had come to talk to him and he was dismissing me?

"Dad. I really need to talk to you about this."

"I know what I'm doing, Floyd. I know you think you're helping. But I don't need you judging me right now. I'm doing what I think is best for the rez."

"But, Dad —"

"Floyd!" he shouted, stunning me into silence. "I'm the adult here! I'm also the Chief! You need to back off and let me do my job!"

I sat there staring at him. My dad wasn't a yeller. He had never yelled at me. And he had *never* talked down to me. But that was exactly what he was doing now.

"Dad —" I tried one more time.

But my father turned around and walked out of his office without another word. He walked away from me without looking back once.

I watched him go. Then I pulled out my cellphone, and called Charlie.

"Hey. It's me. Grab Jasper and Mouse and meet me at my place. Yeah, right now."

Dear Diary

Dear Journal

To Whom It May Concern

Captain's Log — Stardate 2017

Oh forget it. I'm just going to write.

I'm watching my dad, who has always been an amazing role model — not just for me but for everyone on the rez — and I'm watching him crash and burn, spiralling into despair. Poetic maybe. But true.

Why won't he let me help? I have so many ideas! So many ways that I want to help our people. So many ways I think I can help our kids. Why won't he listen?

Doesn't he trust me?

The guys and I want to help before we lose anyone else. I want to help him before he falls apart completely.

He tells me to be a leader. Why won't he let me try?

The guys were already waiting on my front porch when I got home. I let them in and motioned for them to follow me to my room. I knew we'd be alone. My mom was making arrangements for Mary's funeral and my dad was probably showing Feldman around the rez. It made my blood boil just thinking about that has-been trying to cash in on our tragedy.

I had tried to do the right thing and talk to my father. More than once. He wouldn't listen. If he wouldn't listen to me, I'd find another way to get his attention.

I told the guys what the plan was. They loved it. It appealed to Charlie's sense of justice. And Jasper was up for anything that caused chaos.

Even if it was a little like anarchy.

I led the guys into the basement. It was where my mom had packed away and stored every single thing we had ever owned, at my dad's insistence. My dad was a pack rat. He kept everything.

I pulled things out of boxes and handed them around. I took one thing back and replaced it with another. I adjusted things here and there.

We were almost perfect.

Almost.

We needed to get out of the basement and head upstairs. The last thing we needed would be in my mom's room. I sent the guys ahead and turned toward Mouse. He had spent the past half hour hovering around us on the outskirts of the action.

"You okay, buddy?" I asked.

"I guess," Mouse said. He wouldn't look at me. He picked at a fleck of paint on the wall with a fingernail.

"You sure?"

"Yeah. No. I don't know."

"What is it?" I asked him gently.

"Why didn't I get some of that stuff?" he asked. He gestured at the boxes I had been tearing through.

I felt awful that I had left him out without explaining. "Mouse, I'm really sorry. I should have talked to you before we started getting ready. I wasn't trying to leave you out, buddy. But there is a pretty good chance that we're going to get in a lot of trouble over this. Like . . . a *lot* of trouble. I don't want you being part of it. I'd feel terrible if you got into trouble because of me. Do you understand?"

Mouse nodded, wiping at his eyes. That small motion made my heart hurt. I just couldn't dismiss him after that.

"There is one thing though. It's probably the most important thing. It won't get you into any trouble, but we couldn't do this without your help," I told him.

"Really?" he asked.

"For sure. Are you up for it?"

"Yeah! Of course. What do I do?"

"We need a scout. A good one. We need someone to go ahead of us and make sure the coast is clear. We need you to keep anyone from seeing us before we get to the community centre. Do you think you can do that?" I looked him in the eye.

He looked back at me, nodding his head seriously. "Yeah. Definitely. I'll go out now and start looking around, okay?" He leaped to his feet and took two steps toward the stairs.

"Wait!" I called out, bringing him to a dead stop.

"What?"

"You need to wear something dark . . . so you blend in," I told him. "You know . . . like a disguise."

His face lit up. "Yeah! But . . . I don't have anything but this." He looked down at his yellow t-shirt.

"Don't worry, buddy. I've got you covered." I dug back into one of the boxes.

I got Mouse sorted and sent him out to do some recon. Then I headed upstairs.

Charlie and Jasper followed me into my mom's room and watched as I picked her makeup bag up off her dresser. I pulled out a couple of things and turned to look at the guys.

"So . . . who wants to go first?" I asked.

I handed a couple of tubes and pots to Charlie. He got to work on Jasper while I jotted down ideas about what I wanted to say.

Chapter 22
READY FOR BATTLE

As the time for the meeting drew near, a steady stream of people wandered toward the entrance to the community centre. Parents shook hands with the Council members and called out to friends and neighbours. Teenagers shuffled along behind the parents who had dragged them there, acting tough and bored. Small children were carried by their mothers or allowed to run wild like little wâpos, or rabbits.

Mouse was darting around. He hid behind trees and ducked behind a dumpster. He threw elaborate hand signals back toward where Jasper, Charlie, and I were waiting out of sight.

People were shouting greetings back and forth. "Tânisi!" from Auntie Martha. *Hello! How are you?* And a shouted "Miyo takosin!" back from Raynetta. *It's a fine night.* Everyone on the rez loved a good gathering, no matter what the reason. Even in the midst of an epidemic. It was another excuse for the women to gossip to each other and the men to brag about their latest escapades with a hunting rifle, a new truck, or a woman.

From our hiding spot, I watched everyone make their way into the centre. I saw Raynetta walk by with Kaya. I felt my heart stop. Kaya was wearing a yellow sundress and had her hair loose around her shoulders. She looked beautiful. I wasn't sure how she was going to feel about me after this.

There was Chief Burnstick, head of our tribal police. He wasn't a big guy but there was something about him that screamed "authority figure." I had never been in trouble but some of my friends had and they all respected the Police Chief. He treated people fairly and tried to steer them away from trouble if possible. He was younger than you might think a Police Chief would be . . . around forty. But Chief Burnstick's dad had once been Police Chief and his grandfather had been too. So it was kind of his birthright. Just like being hereditary Chief was mine.

After most of the people had filed into the building, Mouse popped up and signalled back at us.

"I think he's telling us to steal home," Charlie quipped. I nodded at Mouse and took a deep breath. *Here we go*, I thought. Charlie, Jasper, and I sidled along the outside wall. We peered into the nearest window. The Council members were sitting on the stage, watching everyone take their seats. I could see my father talking to a short white man in blue jeans, a rip-off Beatles t-shirt, and what looked like an odd assortment of turquoise and silver buckles, bracelets, and chokers. It was Kevin Feldman, B-list star of cheesy made-for-TV movies and heartthrob of, well, nobody that I knew. He looked like a complete dick. He smiled at my father and placed a friendly hand on his shoulder, laughing in what was supposed to be a humble way. *Wow*. He really had the Hollywood networking thing down to an art, phony laugh and all. And there was my dad, tribal elder, hereditary Chief, respected member of our community. And he was about to make a complete fool of himself.

My dad moved toward the microphone. He held up his hands, calling the meeting to order.

"Miyo takosin! Good evening. Thank you all so much for joining us. It shows how much we value our community and how strongly we all want it to succeed," he said. There were a few nods from the older people in the crowd. But most of the audience stared at him without real interest and, in some cases, with outright disdain. Clearly word of what he wanted to do had spread. I felt my face burn with embarrassment for him. I couldn't let him do this. I hated that he wouldn't listen to me but I couldn't stand anyone looking at him like that. He was still our Chief. And he was still my dad.

Mouse gave us the nod. The coast was clear. It was go time.

My dad went on. "As you know, the problems that our children and our community face as a whole is one of the issues I work hard to . . ." His voice trailed off as he caught sight of Jasper, Charlie, and me entering the room. Heads turned to see what he was staring at so intently and gasps went up as the adults registered the scene before them. The teenagers and kids laughed and pointed as Charlie, Jasper, and I strode into the room.

We looked neither right nor left and strode to the front of the room. We stopped in front of the stage and I glared as menacingly as I could at our 'special guest.' Kevin Feldman's mouth was hanging open. He was clearly at a loss for words.

I tossed my braided hair over my shoulder, setting the eagle feather placed into the back dancing. My face was fierce, painted as it was with my mom's lipstick and eyeliner and an old watercolour set I had found in one of the boxes. One side of my face was stark white with a bear claw drawn in black under my eye. The other side was black and featured red tribal symbols of strength and power. At least that's what the images were according to Jasper, who claimed to know a lot about these things. A beaded choker that I had borrowed from my mother's room was around my throat. I wore an old bone breastplate that I had found in the basement over my naked chest.

My friends were painted and costumed too, and the overall effect was, I thought, pretty startling. We stood there in a line, dragging the attention away from my dad.

My father looked confused. He clearly had no idea what we were doing. He started to walk toward us. He could clearly tell it was me and my friends. For a split second, I felt bad about showing him up this way. But this wasn't about him. It was about saving our people. I looked from my dad to the guest of honour. I raised a hand toward Feldman and uttered one word.

"How!"

Pandemonium erupted. The audience went wild with laughter. Even Kevin Feldman was laughing. He was clapping my father on the back. It looked like he thought this was some kind of traditional welcome. Some sort of honour. I thought it again.

What a dick.

Jasper and Charlie stood beside me but out of the corner of my eye I caught a glimpse of Mouse slinking along the wall. I gathered strength from my friends and took a deep breath. I stepped forward until I was standing right in front of my dad and his guest.

I pointed at Feldman. It stopped his laughter pretty much right away. He looked at my dad nervously and then back at me.

"Floyd," my father began. *This isn't about him*, I reminded myself. I didn't even glance at the person responsible for this whole debacle — the Chief, my dad.

Chapter 23
FACE TO FACE

Kevin Feldman's mouth was hanging wide open. I stopped in front of him, feeling Jasper and Charlie move in behind me to flank me on either side. I stared him down, letting him take us in, before I launched into my speech.

"Is this what you want?" I demanded, gesturing at myself. "You want us to dress up in your idea of Native clothes and prance around, talking in some phony accent? I don't know if you're disrespectful or just ignorant. But this is not who we are.

"You've come here to talk us into letting you make a movie about our people. But you don't know us. You want us to embody a cliché to make you look noble. You look at us and you see people who are suffering. People who seem to be in the perfect position — desperate enough to let themselves be taken advantage of. You think if you throw money at us, you'll get what you want. You say you want to bring money to the poor Indians. But at what cost? So you can cash in on what you think people want to see. But we're strong and we're proud of who we are. We don't need a Hollywood has-been to take advantage of us to make a buck.

"If we let you make your movie here, you'll kill our forest and destroy our resources. You won't give a second thought to the mess you'll leave behind for us to clean up. We may not have much but we're proud of where we live. We're proud of our culture. Nothing you can say and no amount of money you can throw at us will make us turn our backs on our culture or our home.

"We're dealing with serious issues that you can't possibly see from your Hollywood Hills office. We will not allow you to profit off of our tragedy. I watch the news. People care about what's happening. If we reach out, we'll be able to reclaim our home without giving up what's most important to us. Go back to Hollywood, Kevin Feldman. We don't need or want you here."

I took in the look of horror on my father's face before I turned my back on Feldman. A roar of applause rose from everyone else in the room. Jasper and Charlie were grinning widely. I saw Mouse back near the entrance, jumping up and down. Holding my head high, I led the way out, followed by Charlie and Jasper.

As soon as I got outside, I was tackled by my friends. Jasper all but climbed onto my back. Charlie high fived me so hard he left my hand stinging. Mouse came flying around the corner — he must have come out the back. He jumped into the air when he was still about six feet away, hurling himself at me and throwing his arms around my neck.

"Floyd! That was amazing!" he yelled.

"Yeah, it was," Jasper agreed. "Seriously. That was awesome."

"You said everything we all wanted to say," Charlie added.

"Yes, you did," said another voice.

I looked up. There was a steady stream of people coming out of the community centre.

"I'm glad someone said something," another voice called out.

People were slapping me on the back and thanking me. I knew my friends and I couldn't be the only ones who thought having Kevin Feldman here was a bad idea. But I had no idea how many people — particularly grown-ups — felt the same.

Charlie and Jasper were basking in the attention, accepting congratulations and handshakes. Mouse was telling anyone who would listen that he was the scout and was in on the whole thing. I shook so many hands that I lost track of who was in front of me.

In the middle of it all, I caught sight of my dad standing inside the doorway, watching the commotion. I was trying to decide if I should go talk to him when his eyes met mine. Before I could decide what to do, I saw his eyes narrow. He turned away and walked back into the community centre.

I had done the right thing. I knew I had. Someone needed to take a stand. I hoped I would remember the look on Kevin Feldman's face for the rest of my life.

And I hoped someday I would forget the look on my father's face as he turned his back on me.

Chapter 24
CHIEF TO CHIEF

It took us a while to extricate ourselves from the crowd of people offering their thanks and support. Everyone had heard about Kevin Feldman's plan and it didn't look like anyone other than my father had actually liked it.

I should have been happy. I should have been revelling in this moment. But all I could think about was the look on my father's face.

I didn't want to go home. But I was wearing a bone breastplate and nothing underneath it. Truth be told, it was chafing a bit. Jasper's house was closest, so we headed over there. I tried to tune out the sound of the guys rehashing the whole thing ad nauseum.

"Did you see Feldman's face?" Jasper asked, jumping around in front of us.

"His mouth was hanging down around his knees!" Charlie crowed.

"That was awesome!" Mouse yelled, pumping his fist in the air.

I tried to smile. I really did. I knew that what we had done was pretty huge. We had stood up for ourselves and for everyone else who thought making a Hollywood movie here was a bad idea. We had done the right thing. But I also knew that I had hurt my dad.

I had embarrassed him. I had ruined what he had planned to help us all.

And I'd have to face him eventually.

I pulled off the chest plate and tossed it down on Jasper's bed.

"That's better," I breathed. "Do you have a t-shirt or something I can borrow?"

"I'm never taking this thing off, man." Charlie patted his own chest plate. "The ladies loved it! Did you see Amber? She was all over me!" He flopped down on Jasper's bed. He stretched out and put his arms behind his head, crossing one leg over the other.

"I saw it, Charlie," Mouse told him.

"Everyone thought you were pretty cool too, buddy." I smiled at Mouse and he beamed back. I wish I felt half as good about myself as Mouse felt about me.

Jasper threw me a t-shirt. I held it up. The Incredible Hulk. Nice. I pulled it over my head. It was a little short but it would get me home.

"You okay, Floyd?" Charlie asked, suddenly picking up on my mood.

"Yeah, I'm good. It was great, right?"

The guys went back to rehashing everything. But I had to go home. I knew that my dad would be waiting for me. Staying at Jasper's house was just putting off the inevitable.

"Guys, I've gotta go," I announced.

"What? You can't leave. We're celebrating!" Charlie said. He propped himself up on one elbow and stared at me.

"I know. But I have to go home. I need to talk to my dad."

×　×　×

When I got near our house, I could see my father sitting in his chair through the front window. I stopped and watched him. His shoulders were slumped. He looked miserable. And I was the cause of it.

I briefly thought about going through the back. Maybe I could climb through my bedroom window and avoid talking to him. But I had stood up to Kevin Feldman for everyone else. I had to stand up to my dad for myself. I couldn't hide. I was the hereditary chief. And a chief wouldn't run away. I squared my shoulders and walked up the front stairs.

"Hi, Dad."

He didn't move. He didn't even look up.

"I know you're upset. But we should talk," I told him.

Nothing. Not even a twitch.

"Dad! You have to talk to me!"

That got his attention. He looked up at me slowly. I hadn't noticed the drink in his hand until he put it down on the side table, ice cubes clinking. He stood and stepped forward until he was looking down at me. My dad had never been that aggressive with me before. But I stood my ground.

"You humiliated me," he said.

"I know. I'm sorry for that," I told him.

"Kevin Feldman is going somewhere else to shoot his movie."

"Well . . . good."

My dad stopped. "What?" he asked. The smell of booze was coming out of his pores.

I refused to take a step back. "We don't need him, Dad. He just wanted to use us. He would have destroyed our land. We need *real* help here, Dad."

"I was going to get that! With the money he brought in. The media would have been all over this."

"What media? *TMZ*? Feldman makes terrible movies to try to get back his minute of fame. He's a joke, Dad. A punchline. It's the wrong kind of attention."

"I was doing what needed to be done."

"No you weren't," I argued. "You were doing what *you* thought needed to be done. But you weren't listening to anyone else!"

"I was listening to the Council!" he yelled.

"No, Dad. You weren't. Because they walked out of the meeting with everyone else and thanked us. I said what everyone else was thinking but were too afraid to say."

"And just what made you think anyone wanted to say that?" he asked.

"All the people high fiving me after! Someone needed to say it, Dad. Someone had to tell Feldman that we aren't here to be scenery for his stupid movie."

"Humpfff," was my dad's only answer. He sat down and picked up his drink again.

"It just should have been you who said it to him." I turned and walked away without another word.

Dear Journal,

When I was younger, my father sent me on a vision quest. It's not something that's done much anymore. But since he is hereditary chief, and I will be after him, my dad thought I deserved to at least try. I went out in the woods and I fasted and sang songs and made offerings.

I didn't see a thing.

I spent three days out there and finally gave up. I was starving and exhausted and had bug bites all over. So I made my way back toward home, wondering if I should make something up to tell my father. I was hereditary chief! I should have encountered some kind of spirit animal or something!

I was just about to step out of the forest and onto the road when I saw a bear. It was standing in the river about ten feet from me. I stopped dead. His strong, musky scent washed over me and I watched as he reached into the river and pulled out a fish. He was about to take a bite when he looked up and noticed me watching him. He sniffed the air and snuffled at me, staring.

I didn't dare move. I just stood and watched him as he took a couple of lumbering steps toward me. He stopped again, right in front of me. He could have reached out his massive clawed paw and swiped at me, spilling my blood all over the ground.

But he didn't.

He made a low sound in his throat. It wasn't a growl.
It sounded more like a greeting.

Stupid, I know.

He stared at me a moment longer. Then he dropped his fish at my feet and turned away. He disappeared into the forest behind me.

My father asked me when I got home if I'd had a vision.

I told him I hadn't.

*He nodded and said that not many people do. He told me
not to worry about it. Maybe I could try again in
a year.*

*I never told my dad about the bear. It seemed like my
moment somehow, like it would take something away to
share it with him.*

*So I walked into the kitchen without a word and handed my
mother the fish.*

Chapter 25
DOWNHILL

I noticed three things over the next few days.

First, that my father was drinking more. He had never been much of a drinker. He had seen what drinking did to a family. His dad had left residential school with a raging drug and alcohol habit. My dad refused to be like his father, he said. He didn't want to be an alcoholic who killed himself during an alcohol-fueled night with a gun he had given his grandson as a gift. I had been cured of any interest in drinking that night. But I guess my father hadn't.

Second, nothing had changed. Kevin Feldman had left the rez with his tail tucked between his legs. But none of our problems were being solved. My dad didn't even seem to have anything in the works. His grand plan to bring Hollywood to the rez had blown up in his face — due in no small part to me. And he didn't have a backup plan. He had taken no steps to get any funding, bring in support, or create programs for us. Nothing.

And third, he was depressed. He was skipping Council meetings. He was sleeping late and spending most of his day sitting in front of the TV, flipping between talk shows and the shopping channel. I wasn't convinced he was even showering. I was getting worried about him, so I mentioned it to my mom. She said he was just stressed out and he'd be fine. I didn't want to think my mom was lying to me, but I wasn't as sure as she was.

And I had noticed a fourth thing.

I was falling in love with Kaya.

The more time I spent with her, the more I liked her. And the more time I spent without her, the more I realized how much I wanted to be around her. All the time. She made me feel good. She made it feel like none of this other stuff was happening. She made me feel normal again. I felt like I had before I found Aaron's body.

I was sitting in Kaya's backyard on one of the old rusted swings. I'd idly push myself with the toe of one sneaker and occasionally swing sideways into Kaya who was on the matching swing.

"Stop that." She mock-frowned and leaned in to kiss me on the cheek. I loved when she did that. I was about to go for a real kiss when she stood up.

"Everything okay?" I asked her. She was frowning but for real this time. But she still looked beautiful and I was thinking about just standing up and grabbing her for that kiss.

"Not really," she said. "I don't know."

"What is it?"

She sighed. Even that was cute. I was definitely a goner. *Focus, Floyd.*

"It's Mouse."

Suddenly she had my full attention. "Is he okay?" I asked.

"I don't know. He hasn't been himself lately, you know? You know he's had trouble with the kids at school and he's starting to stress out about going back. The closer we get to school starting, the worse he is. Some of the kids here have been giving him a hard time, too. They make fun of him for being so small."

"Yeah. I know. They always have. But the guys and I always had his back. Except . . ." I looked away guiltily. "Well, I've been hanging out with you most of the time lately."

"Yeah, I know. I think he feels like we've all forgotten him or something," Kaya said, looking sad. "He's been kind of quiet and withdrawn."

"Mouse has been quiet?" Mouse almost never stopped talking.

"Yeah. He has. I'm worried about him. He's been spending a lot of time in his room. And he's never really done that before. He usually likes to be wherever the rest of the family is."

I didn't know what to think. I felt terrible. Since I had started dating Kaya, I hadn't had much time for anything other than her. I hadn't even taken Mouse out fishing for Rodney again.

"Okay. I'll talk to him," I told her.

"You will?"

"Of course. Just as soon as I get a chance. Maybe I can take him out fishing or something."

"Thank you!" She threw her arms around my neck and kissed me. I would have talked to Mouse without Kaya being so grateful. But this was definitely an added bonus. I kissed her back, brushing a strand of hair off her face and tucking it behind her ear.

There was more kissing after that.

A lot more.

I fully intended to talk to Mouse later that day. I did.

But then Kaya and I spent half the day wrapped around each other. And then the guys came over to talk about an outing that was being planned at the lake for the next day. Then Kaya's parents came out with a jug of lemonade and some of Raynetta's homemade banana bread.

Eventually I left to help my mom make dinner, walking down the road and whistling. It had been a good day and I was looking forward to hanging out at the lake the next day with my friends.

I got home and swung up the stairs. I was opening the door and walking in before I remembered that I hadn't talked to Mouse.

And I hadn't seen him all day either.

× × ×

If I was writing a story about a perfect day at the lake, this is exactly what I would have written. The sun was shining off the water. We had dragged down coolers full of drinks, sandwiches, and snacks and were eating, chatting in groups, or throwing around Frisbees and footballs. Sunscreen-covered girls were flirting, reading magazines, and splashing around at the edge of the water in shorts and bikini tops.

Kaya and I were cuddled up on a blanket, talking about things we wanted to do with the rest of the summer. It was starting to sink in that she'd be going back to school soon. I'd be entering my senior year of high school, drowning in homework. I wanted to make sure we made the most out of the time we had left.

Charlie had finally convinced Amber to go out with him. It was going well, if you could judge by the way he seemed to be sucking her face off.

It was another perfect day.

"Floyd, we're playing touch football in the water. Wanna play?" Jasper asked, running past with Ben and a few other guys.

"Go." Kaya shoved my shoulder.

"You sure?"

"Yeah. I want to catch up with Amber. I'm dying to know what she sees in Charlie." She grinned.

"Hey!" Charlie splashed her with his bottled water.

"Kidding!" she laughed. "Just go, you guys. I need some girl time."

"All right. Be back in a little while, okay?" I kissed her, tasting her strawberry lip gloss and spearmint toothpaste. She winked at me and turned to Amber, who was sending Charlie off with a smack on the ass. Sweet.

I was running down to the water when I caught a glimpse of Mouse. He was sitting by himself on the outskirts of the party. His arms were wrapped around his knees. He was staring down at the sand and the hole he was digging with one foot. I skidded to a stop.

I tossed the ball to Charlie and told him, "Be down in a second," nodding toward Mouse.

Charlie caught the ball and threw it to Jasper, who fumbled. "All right. Hurry up or I'll be stuck on a team with butterfingers over there."

I walked over to where Mouse was sitting. He didn't seem to be aware of anything or anyone around him. "Mouse?" I said softly.

He glanced up at me. "Hi, Floyd." He looked back down at his feet.

I crouched down beside him. "You okay, buddy?"

"Yeah. Just watching."

"Your sister is over there. If you wanted to say hi or something."

"Nah."

"Okay. Ummm. I was thinking we should go out fishing again soon. Look for Rodney."

That got his interest. He looked up. "Really? When?" he asked.

"Floyd! Are you coming?" Ben hollered.

I nodded and held up a finger. "In a minute," I called back.

I turned to Mouse again, who was still waiting for an answer. "Right. Fishing. Ummm. I'm not sure. I'll have to find some time. Maybe next week?"

I regretted those words the second they left my mouth. Mouse's face clouded again. "Sure," he said, his eyes dropping back down to the sand.

"Floyd!" Jasper had joined Ben. "Come on!"

"Coming!" I stood up and looked down at Mouse, feeling that I had failed somehow. "So, Mouse? We'll find some time soon, all right?"

He nodded without looking up.

"Okay then. I'll talk to you later."

He didn't even acknowledge me. I felt uneasy but I didn't know what else to do.

"Come on, Floyd. Be on my team," Charlie shouted. "We'll take these losers DOWN!" He did a little dance and I couldn't help but laugh.

"All right, all right!" I ran down to join my friends. Even as I joined the game I knew that I should have stayed behind with Mouse. But ten minutes later, we had forgotten that we were playing "touch" football and were tackling each other into the water.

Ten minutes later I had also forgotten about Mouse sitting all alone on the beach.

Chapter 26
SEARCHING

The theme to *Star Wars* woke me up out of a dead sleep.
I reached for my phone and knocked it to the floor. I grabbed at
it. Once. Twice. I finally got a couple of fingers on it and picked it
up. I squinted at the screen. 1:30? Who'd be calling at 1:30? Kaya's
face was flashing on the screen. Why would Kaya be calling me
at 1:30?

"Kaya?"

She was sobbing on the other end. "Floyd?" That was the only
word I could make out.

"Kaya? What's wrong?"

"Floyd, Mouse is gone."

"What? Where is he?" I was sitting up now.

"I don't know. He's gone. I couldn't sleep. I was worried
about him. I realized I hadn't seen him all night so I went to talk
to him. I thought he might still be awake. But he wasn't there.
His bed was still made. I looked all over the house for him.
I looked outside. He's gone, Floyd." She was crying hard again.

"Did you tell your parents?" I stood up and looked for a
t-shirt.

"Yes. They're out looking for him."

"Okay. That's good."

"He left his sketchbook open on his bed."

"So?"

"You have to see it," she said.

I pulled on a pair of jeans and crouched down, peering under the bed for my sneakers. "I'm on my way over, okay?"

"Okay. But, Floyd?"

"Yeah?"

"One of my dad's guns is missing. Mouse must have taken it."

I felt like someone had forced a hand inside my chest and was squeezing my heart. I sat down hard on the bed, thinking of Mouse and then of Aaron. Aaron had taken off with a gun in the middle of the night. I had gotten a call and had gone looking for him too.

I couldn't stand the thought of finding Mouse like I had found Aaron. I felt sick just thinking about it.

"Okay," I said to Kaya. "It'll be okay. I'm going to wake my parents and get the guys. We'll all look for him, all right?"

"Okay. All right." She took a deep breath. "Floyd, what he drew . . . I'm scared he'll do something . . ." she trailed off.

"I know. I'll find him. I'll be there soon."

I hung up and went into my parent's room. I walked past my dad's side of the bed and shook my mother awake.

"Floyd? What's wrong? Are you sick?" she asked sleepily.

"No. But I need you to get up. And get Dad up too. Mouse is missing. And he took one of John's guns."

My mother was up and out of bed before I had even finished the sentence. She grabbed some clothes and shook my father.

"Go, Floyd," she urged me. "We'll meet you there."

"Okay."

I was dialing my cell before I even closed the door behind me.

"Charlie? It's me. Is Jasper staying with you? Get him up. Meet me at Mouse's right now. He's missing." I was about to hang up and then continued. "And, Charlie? He has a gun."

Charlie hung up without a word. I knew he was already waking Jasper.

I ran to Mouse's house. The entire place was lit up and Kaya was sitting on the front porch. She jumped up and threw herself at me, pressing her tear-soaked face against my chest. She was stabbing me in the neck with what I assumed was Mouse's sketchbook. I hugged her close but pulled away quickly. I needed to get out and look for Mouse.

She held the book out to me. "Look," she said simply.

I didn't have to leaf through too many pages to see that something was wrong. At the beginning of the book, Mouse's drawings were colourful and vivid and full of life. They were pretty amazing actually. But closer to the end of the book they got dark. Disturbing. Sad. He switched out his coloured pencils and markers for black ink and charcoal. One picture showed a boy sitting in a corner with his knees drawn up to his chest and his face hidden in his arms. There were people standing over him, laughing.

The next page wasn't any better. On it the same boy was sinking, reaching toward the surface of the water and screaming.

I turned another page and saw the boy again. It was Mouse — I could see his face clearly in this one. He was standing in the rain, looking utterly hopeless. I couldn't look away from his face. He had drawn himself with no life left in his eyes.

I closed the book and handed it back to Kaya. My heart was somewhere down around my sneakers.

"I'm going to look for him. You stay here in case he comes back," I told Kaya. "I'm heading down to the lake. Charlie and

Jasper will be here soon. Send them out in the other direction, okay? I'll have my phone with me. Call me if you hear anything."

"I will."

I kissed her forehead and left, heading down toward the lake. I rushed toward the same area where I had found Aaron. I was wishing with all my might that history wouldn't repeat itself tonight.

The woods were dark and my flashlight lit up just a few feet in front of me. I was going hoarse yelling Mouse's name at the top of my lungs. It got brighter and my heart beat faster the closer I got to the lake. I was terrified that I'd find Mouse just like I had found Aaron. I couldn't handle that again.

"Mouse!" I yelled, as I stepped into the clearing and ran down the beach. Where was he? I looked in the spot he had been the last time we were at the lake. It was empty. I checked my phone. Nothing. No one had found him yet or they would have let me know.

I walked aimlessly. Despite myself, despite my growing desperation . . . or maybe because of it . . . I started coming up with a story in my head.

Once upon a time there was a little mouse who wanted to fit in. Wherever the bigger mice would go, he would follow. He ran after them, trying to get their attention. But they were too busy with their own big mouse lives to notice him.

The little mouse tired himself out chasing after the bigger mice. He nibbled at their ankles to make them notice him. But the bigger mice just ran faster, chasing girl mice and having mouse adventures without him.

Feeling rejected, the lonely little mouse finally gave up. He found a quiet spot by the water where he could curl up and hide.

The bigger mice kept running around. But soon they noticed that no one was nipping at their ankles. No one was asking questions or trying to get in on their adventures. One by one, they stopped running and looked around.

"Where's the little mouse?" one of them asked.

"Wasn't he just behind us?" another guessed.

"I haven't seen him in a while," said a third mouse.

The bigger mice were worried. They couldn't remember a time when the little mouse wasn't chasing after them. They started looking for him. They ran across the fields, calling his name. They looked under logs and ran over rocks, calling his name.

But the little mouse didn't answer.

I knew I could never write down the story unless it had a happy ending. And the story didn't have a happy ending because the stupid bigger mouse forgot that the little mouse was there and never did talk to him or take him fishing. Because he's an idiot.

Damn.

I turned in circles, looking for my friend but it was hopeless.

He wasn't here. I turned around and started to head back into the darkness of the forest. I walked toward the tree line and then stopped suddenly.

I *was* an idiot.

I knew where he was.

I turned away from the woods and headed down the beach at a full run.

Chapter 27
FOUND

I was out of breath and had a stitch in my side by the time I got there. I arrived at the dock where the fishing boat was tied up. Mouse was sitting on the end, his feet dangling over the edge. He was looking down at something in his lap.

His dad's gun.

I slowed down, not wanting to startle him.

"Mouse?" I called out gently.

He looked over. He turned his head to watch me walking up the lake's edge toward him.

"It's me. Floyd."

"Floyd?" Mouse's voice was shaking. He was crying.

"Yeah, buddy. Can I come and sit with you?"

He shrugged. I took that for a yes. I walked down the dock and lowered myself carefully beside him. I saw the gun in his hand and tried not to stare at it. We'd get to that in a minute.

"How are you doing, Mouse? Are you okay?"

"No," he broke down. "I'm tired of it, Floyd."

I put a hand on his back. "Tired of what, buddy?"

"Tired of being made fun of and teased all the time. I try to laugh. And not care. But I do. I hate it. They push me around. I don't know how to fight back when they're so much bigger than I am. School's about to start and I don't think I can take another year of that."

I nodded. I had been called names and dealt with the racist bullshit at school. But no one had ever dared push me around for long. But I understood how he felt. "Remember I told you that the kids made fun of my hair?" I asked.

"Yeah."

"Well, I didn't tell you that they made fun of my clothes sometimes, too. We couldn't afford new school clothes one year. I was wearing an old pair of jeans with holes in the knees and a t-shirt my dad had meant to throw out. They called me a dirty Indian and said we were on welfare. They said my dad was a drunk. We weren't on welfare, and Dad didn't drink. Not then. But they didn't bother to see past the way I looked. They saw what they thought was a poor kid from the rez and made fun of me. Which was pretty stupid. I *was* a poor kid from the rez but that wasn't all I was. You know? It didn't make them any better than me."

"But didn't it bother you?"

"Of course. It bothered me a lot. I punched one of them. The one who had called me a dirty Indian."

"But they're bigger than me," Mouse said sadly. "If I fight them, I'll get hurt."

"You shouldn't have to fight, Mouse. Believe me, I can't fight everyone who I think deserves it. My mom taught me that violence is never the answer. I know you can't just ignore them. But you can learn to protect yourself. I'll help you. And this year you'll be in high school. With me."

"Yeah?" There was a hint of hope in his voice.

"Yeah. And Charlie and Jasper and Ben too. We're not going to let anyone bully you, Mouse. It'll get easier. I promise. Fighting isn't the answer. And neither is that," I said. I nodded down at the gun in his hand.

"I know, Floyd," he murmured. "I didn't really want to die. I just . . . I didn't know what else to do. I just wanted it to stop."

"Yeah," I said. I knew that was how Aaron must have felt that night in the woods. I couldn't stop it that night but I could now. "But maybe if you feel this way again you can talk to me about it. I know I haven't been here for you as much as I should have. And I'm sorry for that, Mouse. I got caught up with Kaya and didn't realize how badly you needed help. That won't happen again. I promise."

"Okay," he said simply.

I reached over and took the gun. I put it down beside me and slung an arm across Mouse's shoulders.

"I wasn't there for Aaron. And I haven't been there for you. But I will be. And if you ever feel like this again, you call me. No matter what time it is. It'll be like the Bat signal," I told him, trying to make him smile. "You call and I'll be there." I hugged him hard against my side.

"I will, Floyd. Thanks."

"You don't have to thank me, buddy. We're friends."

He hugged me back.

In a bit, I stood and offered him a hand. I pulled him up to his feet.

"I have to call everyone and let them know you're okay," I explained. "There are a lot of people out looking for you. We all care about you, Mouse."

He smiled a little at that. I was grateful I had the chance to tell him. I had been too late to tell Aaron that I loved him like a brother and didn't care if he was gay. I wasn't going to make that kind of mistake again.

"Come on. Let's get you home," I said. I left my arm around his shoulder and let him talk the whole way back.

Dear Self — who is, hopefully, older and wiser than I was yesterday,

I haven't believed in happy endings for a really long time. Hard to think things are going to end well when the people you love keep dying.

Or showing how human they are.

But I found Mouse before he did something he couldn't take back and we lost him forever. That's about as happy an ending as I can imagine.

I can't imagine waking up to a world without Mouse in it.

I can't imagine finding another friend dead by the water.

I can't imagine having to deal with the fact that I failed another person I love.

Luckily, this time I didn't have to.

Mouse told me that he didn't really want to die. I believe him. But he needs a friend that he can rely on and who has his back. He needs to know that someone cares about him.

I failed to be the friend he needs. But I'll never fail him again.

I came close to losing him like I lost Aaron.

It's time I start trying to fix what's wrong with our community. It's time to help my friends find a place they can belong and be proud of.

It's time to step up and realize that I don't have to wait until I'm older to start acting like a chief. The first step was standing up to my father and making him see that there are things we can do. Things I can do. If he won't respect me enough to listen, then I'll have to make him respect me.

My friends and I, all of us, we have a future. It's about time we took control of it.

Chapter 28
BEING A MAN

I walked back with my arm tightly around Mouse's shoulders. I wasn't sure I'd ever be able to let him go again. But I didn't have a choice when I got him back home. He was all but torn away from me before we even crossed the yard. John ran across the yard so fast I was afraid he wasn't going to be able to stop. But he screeched to a halt and grabbed Mouse away from me, throwing his arms around his son and crying loudly.

"I'm sorry, Dad," Mouse said, stretching his arms around his huge father.

"We'll take care of this, son. We're going to talk about it and figure things out, okay? And if you ever need to talk, you come to me." Tears were streaming down his face as he hugged his son tightly.

Raynetta came out of the house and saw John and Mouse in the yard. With a scream, she flew down the stairs and ran to them. She grabbed Mouse and kissed him repeatedly. She was crying and hugging him like she never wanted to let him go.

I knew how she felt.

But this was a private moment. I had already called Jasper and Charlie to let them know that Mouse was okay. I was about to turn around and leave Raynetta and John alone with their son.

"Floyd?" It was Kaya.

I turned and smiled at her. "Told you I'd bring him back," I said, giving her a quick hug. She kept sneaking looks over my shoulder at her brother. "Go." I smiled and nodded toward Mouse.

She smiled back and kissed me super-fast. Then she ran to her family and wiggled her way into the group hug to get to her brother.

✕   ✕   ✕

If the awful experience with Mouse had taught me one thing it was that life was short. Obviously I knew that. Look at Aaron. But I had been trying to get my dad to listen to me for months, and had failed. We had almost lost Mouse because no one was doing anything to make things better for us. I couldn't let that happen again. It was time to make my dad listen. It was time to start working toward a better life for us here.

My father was in the kitchen when I got home. I had no thought of sneaking into my bedroom this time. I had put this off long enough.

My dad must not have been home for long. There was a fresh drink sitting in front of him on the table. I watched him pick up the glass and swirl the ice cubes around before taking a huge gulp.

"Dad?" I stepped into the kitchen and stood across from him.

He looked up at me blearily. It wasn't so much that it was the middle of the night as it was the fact that it clearly wasn't his first drink. I felt a flash of anger.

"Floyd?"

"Yeah. We need to talk."

"About what?" He looked like his eyes wouldn't quite focus.

"Put your drink down, Dad. We need to talk. Now."
My tone must have shocked him into doing what I said. He put his drink down and stared at me.

I started before he could get a word out. "Mouse almost died tonight. This place, our home, is dying around you. And you're doing nothing about it. You're letting it die. You're letting our people die. I've watched you drowning in alcohol these past few weeks. I've watched you sink into depression. You can't lead us like this, Dad. We need a leader. And you need help. You need to step down and let someone else lead for a while. You need to get healthy. Take care of yourself and let someone else take care of everything else for a while."

"I'm fine," he protested.

"You're not. You're turning into everything you always swore you wouldn't be." I looked at him hard. "You're turning into your father."

I watched the colour drain from my father's face. I wasn't trying to hurt him and I felt bad. But that lasted only a few seconds.

"Dad, Mouse could have died. I could have lost another friend like I lost Aaron. And it was my fault."

I saw him take this in. I didn't want him to get me off track so I kept going before he had a chance.

"It was my fault because I watched him fading away for weeks. He withdrew. He became a ghost of himself. And I was too busy with my friends . . . with Kaya to notice. I let him slip away until he felt like there was no hope left for him. But I got lucky. I found him before it was too late. I got to him before he could do anything . . . before he could kill himself. But next time . . . the next person who feels like they have no future, they might not be so lucky."

My father was staring at me. The words had died on his lips and he was listening to me. He was letting me speak and was actually listening.

"I almost lost another friend. But I won't let that happen again, Dad. I was too busy thinking about myself to be there for Mouse." I took a deep breath. "And you're too busy drinking and sinking into depression to be there for any of us."

"I'm working on getting funding —" he began.

"It's not enough! No amount of money is enough. It's about us. I have ideas, Dad. Good ideas. You had a plan with Kevin Feldman and it didn't work out. You should have moved on. Put it behind you and figured out another way to help. But you're letting it destroy you. We all make mistakes."

"And you think your ideas will be any better than mine?" he challenged.

"I do. And they're not just my ideas. My friends and I have got some great ideas to start healing this community and giving us all something to look forward to."

"I've spent years leading our people," my father said. He looked longingly at his drink. "Do you really think a bunch of kids can come up with an idea that I didn't think of?"

"Yes. We want to open up the community centre again. Start celebrating our culture again instead of drowning in it."

"How are you going to get the money for that?"

"We don't need it . . . not at first anyway. Everyone could pitch in and help. We have enough talent and knowledge right here. Our elders can teach us our language. They can help everyone learn to hunt and fish and find things in the forest. We could have classes in traditional arts like beading and dance. And not just the adults. Kids can share what they learn off the rez. Mouse could teach art. Kaya could do some theatre stuff when she's home. Charlie and Jasper both play soccer and lacrosse. We could have storytelling nights and creative writing classes. I could do that."

"You've really given this a lot of thought, haven't you? All of you."

"Yeah, Dad. We did. I know it's not going to be some easy fix. All of our problems aren't going to be solved overnight. But it's a start."

My dad looked past me, out the window, into the darkness behind me. "I thought that losing the movie would be the end of us. I couldn't see past Kevin Feldman taking his money back to Hollywood." He shifted his gaze to me. "I fell apart. And you're right. I started acting less like me and more like my father."

"But what sets a leader apart is the ability to admit when they're wrong and move forward," I told him.

"You're right. But this time it was you who found a way forward. Not me."

My father was looking down at his glass. Before I could say anything, he stood and walked over to me. He looked at me silently for a long moment. Then he reached out and grasped my shoulder.

"You're going to make a great chief someday, Floyd," he told me. He looked as proud as I had ever seen him.

Chapter 29
WHERE WE ARE

The fish weren't biting as well as they had been the first time Mouse and I had were out. But somehow it didn't matter. We had a huge lunch packed and the sun was shining hotly on the backs of our necks. I was watching Kaya try to put a worm on her hook without dropping it into the lake. She was probably the least girlie girl I knew, but worms totally freaked her out. She always ended up screaming and throwing the wriggling thing over the side. Mouse and I spent more time laughing than actually fishing when the three of us went out.

"So what do you think, Floyd? Any chance we'll get Rodney today?" Mouse asked slyly.

"Mouse! That was supposed to be a secret!" I tossed a worm at him.

He ducked, laughing.

"Hey! There are no secrets on the lake!" Kaya said, gently draping her worm over her hook.

"Your worm is going to drop into the lake as soon as you cast," I told her. "You have to actually thread it onto the hook."

"I can't! I'm not a worm killer."

"She could use one of the sandwiches as bait instead," suggested Mouse. "Maybe peanut butter and jelly." He winked.

The three of us had been doing things together pretty regularly since the night Mouse ran away. Fishing. Hiking in the woods. Hunting — with a camera, not a gun. Hanging out at their place. Or mine. Mouse needed me. He needed us. And we were both there for him without question. We all were.

Mouse was thriving. I had been teaching him how to box. My Nimosôm had taught me when I was a kid. It was one of my best memories of him. He wanted me to always be able to defend myself and I wanted the same for Mouse. I figured it might make him more confident too. I'd dug out my old boxing gloves and the light bag from under some camping gear in the garage. I took the whole mess down to the community centre so I could teach Mouse some moves.

He was actually really good. He had started showing some of the younger kids the basics and they loved him for it.

"Been working on your jab?" I asked him.

"Yeah, a little. More footwork lately though."

"Great," I said. "I finally found that heavy bag too. We can hang that up this weekend."

"Cool. Kaya, maybe I can show you some moves . . . teach you how to protect yourself."

"I'd actually like that, little brother," she said with a smile.

Mouse had started high school where I was around to keep an eye on him. Charlie and Jasper had his back too. But something had changed for Mouse. He didn't seem to need us looking out for him as much as he used to.

Something had changed for a lot of us.

My dad had actually listened to me. He was getting help for his depression, he was going to AA meetings regularly, and he had stepped down for a while to take care of himself. But before he did, he told the Council that I had some good ideas and that they should listen to what I had to say.

They didn't just listen. They let me go ahead and start a youth program at the community centre. The first thing I did was get my friends to clean it up and repaint it inside and out. We made a new sign. Word got out and kids started to come by.

I put together some programs for them . . . sports and cultural activities. We did storytelling and worked on our Cree. We played basketball and lacrosse. I found a career counsellor to come in and talk about colleges and trade schools and funding to help us get an education. The Council finally got some funding for mental health care and helped us however they could.

Charlie and Jasper were teaching kids how to work on cars. They also got enough kids to put a soccer team together. Amber got the girls to play soccer against the guys and they gave us quite a run for our money. Kaya came home from school on weekends now and did workshops on beading and shawl dance for the girls.

And Mouse started teaching a regular workshop on cartooning. He was nervous at first but his excitement about art was contagious. His group of kids were currently working on a graphic novel about life on the reserve. I was writing some of the text. And I wasn't the only one. I had a regular group of kids working on short stories and journals and poetry . . . it was pretty amazing.

The community centre was finally being used by everyone, but what happened next surprised me. A lot of the activities and social events migrated down to the lake. It seemed more appropriate somehow, especially for the kids.

A lot of us had felt alone before. But things had changed when we started these programs at the centre. Now when anyone had a problem or issue, we got together and talked about it around the fire. Eventually we had a regular meeting — a healing circle — where we could share anything we wanted. Nothing was off limits. We talked and we supported each other. We got together and built a sweat lodge with the elders.

And the number of kids trying to kill themselves was going down.

Hugely.

×　×　×

There was a bunch of kids hanging around the dock when we got back.

"Catch anything?" my dad called out. He was crouched at the water's edge, surrounded by kids.

"Nah. They weren't really biting today," Kaya replied.

"No sign of Rodney, Mouse?" he asked.

"Mouse! Is there anyone you haven't told?" I threw a towel at him.

"Sorry! I thought your dad might know where he hung out." He turned back to my dad. "What are you doing?"

"We're collecting water and soil samples."

"Why?"

"We're going to test them and then compare the results with samples from last year."

"We're catching tadpoles too!" A little girl held up a container full of squirmy baby frogs.

"I'll help!" Mouse shoved his tackle box into my already full arms and ran after them.

I knew that it would take more than this to fix all of our problems. But it was a good start. The kids had somewhere to go when things weren't working at home. They had a support system. And the Council was going to start putting together programs for the adults too. My mom was helping. They were hoping to bring down the rate of suicide among the grown-ups like we had for the kids.

We had a long way to go but I had hope. We all had hope.

And that was a pretty good place to start.

Dear Future Floyd,

You're stronger than you think. If you ever doubt yourself again, read this and remember what you accomplished.

Hey, this is Mouse. If I ever feel down again, you should remind me that I helped.

Signed,
Mouse

P.S. I couldn't have done it without you, Mouse.

Chapter 30
WALKING INTO OUR FUTURE

I stepped out of the cool darkness of the community centre and into the quickly fading daylight. I held a hand up to shade my eyes, squinting into the last of the late afternoon sunshine.

Mouse looked up from where he was straightening a pair of moccasins on the ground. I nodded at him and watched as he carefully placed a notecard above the mocs. He stood up and put his hands on his back, stretching backward with a groan like an old man.

"Almost finished," he called out.

"What's left?" I asked.

"Just the last pair at the end." He nodded toward a shopping bag on the ground beside him.

"You got the notecard?"

"Yep. Give me five minutes," he said. He grabbed the bag and headed off down the path at a run.

I watched him go. He had worked hard for this. We both had.

"Floyd?"

I hadn't heard my parents arrive. My mother gave

me a tight hug. My father held out his hand, which I shook. In the past that would have seemed odd: a handshake with my father. But I understood why he offered his hand now. It was his way of showing me that he respected what I was trying to do. What I had already done.

That handshake meant a lot to me.

"Ready?" I asked them. They both nodded.

My mother took my arm and I led them down the path toward the lake.

Mouse had placed pairs of moccasins on either side of the trail from the community centre all the way down to the water. It was a tribute we had come up with to remember the people our rez had lost. My parents and I were the first to walk down that moccasin trail. No one else would see it until tomorrow.

I stopped beside a tiny pair of mocs and read the card Mouse had placed above it.

Abigail Sitting Bear

Abby loved to sing and dance. She had a smile that always made you smile back. She wanted to be a dancer when she grew up. Abby, we'll miss you forever.

Further down the path and across from Abby's mocs was a larger pair. They were intricately beaded and well-worn from years of use — Mary's moccasins. My mother had written the card to go with it. She knelt down and touched the beadwork on the moccasins.

Mary Running Wolf

Auntie Mary was a role model to everyone, a friend and healer to many, and family to me.

Auntie Mary took care of me like I was her own and taught me everything she knew about medicine and healing.

She was the strongest woman I know.

— Cardinal Twofeathers

We walked on, looking to one side of the path, then the other, following the moccasins. There was a pair of large ones that had belonged to one of my dad's friends, another elder. A smaller pair with fur trim belonged to the mother of one of the kids I used to hang out with. We walked the long line of moccasins leading all the way down the lake.

My parents walked silently beside me. They took it all in. I had already seen it when Mouse and I were setting it up, but I still found it pretty overwhelming. We walked slowly down the path, stopping here and there to read a card or study a pair of moccasins, until we reached the end of the trail at the water's edge. There was one spot that had been left empty until now. Mouse was waiting and held out the shopping bag to me without a word.

I pulled out a pair of really cool kicks, Nike running shoes that Aaron had bought about a week before he died. The soles were only lightly scuffed. The blue and orange colours were unmarred by dirt. Aaron had been so proud of those sneakers. It seemed right somehow to display them for Aaron instead of a pair of mocs.

I leaned down and put Aaron's shoes carefully on the edge of the trail. They would sit underneath the card that Mouse had placed there earlier. It was the only card I had written myself.

Aaron

My friend.

My brother.

In this world and the next.

Truly the best of men.

I stood above those words and felt lonelier than I had ever felt in my life. Then my father slipped his arm over my shoulders and reminded me that I wasn't alone.